Storyteller Journal of Wr

Started in 2017

Volume 8 · Issue 12 · April 2024

ISBN: 978-1-955783-01-9

EDITOR
Shay Shivecharan

COPY EDITOR
Michael Birk

ASSOCIATE EDITORS
Gabriel McLeod, Joshua Mahn

COVER PHOTOGRAPHY
Jeannie Albers

FEATURED ON COVER
Londyn Rayne

 threeowlspublishing.com/storytellerjournal

 storyteller@threeowlspublishing.com

 fb.com/storytellerjournal

 @storytellerjournal

Storyteller is a publication of **Three Owls Publishing**

THREE OWLS
PUBLISHING

JEANNIE ALBERS
Art Director & Photographer

JEANNIEALBERS.COM

POETRY

Tonight	*Londyn Rayne*	7
Tethered	*Londyn Rayne*	23
Let the Seeds Sow	*Gabriel McLeod*	25
Reminiscence	*Londyn Rayne*	27
Poems (various)	*Casey Margarite Field*	31
I am the bee	*Clay Waters*	34
The pyrite life	*Clay Waters*	35
Quicksand	*Londyn Rayne*	37
Blue Bottles	*Gabriel McLeod*	38
Gift Shop Dog Toy 1962	*Clay Waters*	39
Blue Soap	*B.T. Shireman*	42
Who's There?	*Clay Waters*	43

FICTION

How to Catch the Ball	*Alan Sincic*	9
Out of Office	*Joshua Mahn*	44
Death or Time Alike	*Joshua Mahn*	46
Gable	*Aaron Morrison*	50
Afterbirth	*Gabriel McLeod*	61
The End of the World	*Alan Sincic*	68
The Greyhound	*Alan Sincic*	80
If You're Cold, They're Cold	*Aaron Morrison*	87
The Smile Contest	*Alan Sincic*	90
No Life Signs : Part 1	*Shay Shivecharan*	106

CONTRIBUTORS

Alan Sincic
A teacher at Valencia College, short stories of mine have appeared in *New Ohio Review*, *The Greensboro Review*, *Boulevard Online*, *The Saturday Evening Post*, *Grist*, *Big Fiction*, *Terrain.org*, and elsewhere. In recent years my fiction and nonfiction have won contests sponsored by *Hunger Mountain*, *Meridian*, *Orison*, *The Texas Observer*, *Driftwood Press*, *The Plentitudes*, *Prism Review*, *Pulp Literature*, *Broad River Review* and others.

 www.alansincic.com

Casey Margarite Field
Casey Margarite is an activist, speaker, author and social entrepreneur who believes in the power of imagination and joy to transform the world. Her heart beats to see her brothers and sisters know their true identity in Christ, find freedom, and imagine beyond their sight. She is a Florida native who loves travel, great coffee, and her golden doodle rescue Maxwell.

 @caseymargarite_

Clay Waters
Clay Waters lived in Florida until the age of four and returned to find it hadn't changed a bit. Three of his six memories from that first stop involve the alphabet, which in retrospect was a bit of a tell. He has had stories and poetry published in The Santa Barbara Review, The Headlight Review, Green Hills Literary Lantern, and Poet Lore, as well as Storyteller.

 @clayman45123

B.T. Shireman
BT is a technologist by profession with a passion for the written word and counts among his influences Bukowski, McCarthy, WB Yeats, Ishiguro and Bradbury. He is a father, painter, wood worker and writer who lives in Central North Carolina.

CONTRIBUTORS

Londyn Rayne

Londyn Rayne is a poet, songwriter and spoken word artist. Often blending words rich in both melancholy and hope, accompanied by a cinematic soundscape for the message to rest in. Bending back and forth between melody and poetry, creativity is her most comfortable form of communication and she uses it to advocate for emotional and mental health and healing. Her debut poetry collection Smokescreen is available now through Three Owls Publishing.

 @londynrayne

Aaron Morrison

Aaron was born during the great __natural disaster__ in the _season_ of _year_. He spends his free time exploring __unusual location__ and raising domesticated __fictional creature(plural)__. One day, he would like to _verb_ his way to _place_ and try the various _noun(plural)_.

 @theaaronmorrison
 linktr.ee/TheAaronMorrison

Gabriel McLeod

Gabriel is an artist and writer that hails from the Deep South and currently resides in a moment of time at a corner of Earth known as Florida. He found meaning through the escape in creativity at an early age and has been chasing that feeling ever since. He is honored to be part of the *Storyteller* family.

 @gabrielmcleod

Joshua Mahn

Joshua Mahn is being pursued by a fearsome beast just outside of your house, immediately after you fall asleep. Please leave some refreshments on the patio suitable for both him and the beast, if you should think of it

 @joshmahnwrites

CONTRIBUTORS

Shay Shivecharan

Shay is a dreamer, through and through. This lifelong affliction has driven him to success at times and caused him to suffer failure at others, and he is grateful for all of it. Though he personally feels most inclined toward writing and music, he holds all art in high regard, especially for the impact it makes on both the artist and any person who encounters it.

◉ @wordsandmusicbyshay

Storyteller is always looking for new voices and fresh perspectives. Submissions can be made to: **storytellersubmissions@gmail.com**

TONIGHT
by Londyn Rayne

my mind
is not kind tonight
I don't know if I can do this

my heart
is nervous tonight
it murmurs with pain
that fills the vacancy
where it's said to be beating
I gasp for breath
and grab my chest
as it aches and re-breaks
i'm sweating and trembling

my hope
is dying alone tonight
initial arrests are cardiac
the attacks are secondary
I react
laying flat
my only stability
is this hard floor like a split
something that supports me
behind my back

my eyes
are burning tonight
after the fight to keep them open
in the straight lines of sustained wind
my sight has swollen shut
yet my tears still drain
down the sides of my cheeks
flooding my ears
until I can't hear
you speak

HOW TO CATCH THE BALL
by Alan Sincic

Step One. Thinking About Catching the Ball

A. Attitude

All your life you have dreamed of catching the ball and now, at last, it is time to begin. You have studied the history of catching, memorized that list of the most famous catchers of the ball, undergone extensive reconstructive surgery to render you more attractive to other catchers of the ball and to the ball-catching community in general.

B. Physical Conditioning

The muscles to be used for the catching of the ball are different than the muscles for throwing. Throwing muscles tend to be large, lug-like, twitching conglomerates of raw red tissue also used for the lifting of fully-loaded boxcars onto railroad sidings or the shoving of four-ton grand pianos through the plate glass windows of expensive French restaurants. Not that throwing is such a – should be such a – big whoop-de-doo. Any spherical object flung out into space in any direction can be considered a *thrown ball*. Any drunken palooka with a pound of raw hamburger in his mitt and a pack of stray dogs snapping at his heels knows what it means to *throw the ball*.

Catching the ball, however, requires a precision and an intelligence few individuals possess. Catching muscles are a set of tiny, finely-tuned filaments, an exquisitely delicate processing system responsive only to the most sophisticated of neural commands. The ball must be snatched from its trajectory at that one – and only one – optimal point of intersection between catcher and catchee. One must calculate to within a fraction of an inch the mutual approach velocities of a matched set of interrelated parabolic arcs. Ergo, catching muscles are intellectual muscles, and the physique of the pure catcher of the ball need not necessarily be anatomically imposing. Here, have another doughnut.

C. What to Eat

In order to be attractive to the ball, it is important for you to look as much like a ball as possible. Since you are what you eat, we suggest as many sphere-icular foods as possible: cheese balls, gumballs, sourballs, crème-puffs, bon-bons, chocolate-covered ho-ho's. Be creative. Don't be afraid to vary your training program by expanding beyond the six major food groups listed here. This is what is known as "having a good range."

Step Two. The Proper Equipment

The glove was first developed in the middle ages to keep the hand warm during the period of time between the catching of the balls. As this period of time grew longer and longer, and the hand grew colder, the glove grew larger, gradually working its way up the arm, over the shoulder, and down across the torso in a linked, lobster-like armor of leather and beaten steel panels. Gloves today are made of space-age high-impact sear-resistant projectile-deflecting materials like Teflon, graphite, titanium, epoxified nano-tubular high-tensile torque-resistant plutonium schmeer – like the one that I am wearing. Meaning: belonging to me. Mine. No touchy-touchy.

But not to worry. Right on your own doorstep you can find everything you need. Do you have a pair of sunglasses? Good. Do you have a pair of cleats? Good. Do you have a pair of shins? Good, good. Then roll up the legs of those city-boy trousers and let's have a *say hey!* Just where have you been hiding those things? Those babies look smooth as a pair of porcelain swizzle sticks. You cannot hope to be catching the ball with equipment like that. Here, here's a bottle of Neatsfoot Oil, trot back down to the trainers room and give those pegs a little rub-down. And here, here's a ball you can pound into those shins a few hundred times so as to make them soft and flexible and responsive to the touch, so as to make them the shins of a true professional. This is what is known as the *breaking in of the equipment*.

Step Three. The Proper Position

Now limp on out to the diamond here so we can get a good look at you. Good. Now get yourself down into the proper position. No, no, that is the fetal position. That is not right, that is incorrect, that is going to result in an *error*. An *error* is what causes you to miss the ball.

Now stand up. Good. Now let go of my hand. Good, good. Let's just try to concentrate on the ball on the ground – the *grounder*. There's the ball. Okay now: catch it! Good, good. Now put it back down again. Okay now, catch it! Good, good! You have mastered the most basic of the fundamental of the skills, the catching of the stationary ball. Now close your eyes and try to visualize what it would be like if there was some kind of a movement on this ball. No, no, do not move the ball! Focus your energies upon the beingness of the ball, the Zen state of the baseballness of the ball. Good, good. Aquinas says that the ball is the same ball whether it is in a state of motion or in a state of rest. Einstein says that time will actually be passing more slowly when the ball is in a state of rest. Feel how slowly the state of time is passing. Good, good. Whew! This is an awful lot to try to grasp hold of here. Here, here is some milk and some cookies, lie down here for a little bit, take yourself a little nap, that's plenty enough for today.

Step Four – Watching The Ball

Here is the ball. Now watch it closely. Watch as we waft it to you gently with a puff of our breath, like a dandelion sailing on a light summer breeze. Watch as it draws closer, as it picks up speed, as it dances erratically to the left and to the right, and spins like a swordfish, pitched by a hurricane, up onto the deck of a greasy Argentinean trawler.

Whoops. Too bad, you missed it. That's an error. But watch, watch, it's circling now for another pass. Here, here is some Dramamine, quick now, before it – *whoops*. Error! Error! That's another error!

This time around let's try to be a bit more precise in our ball-catching technique, shall we? Good. Come out from behind that tree. Good, good. Now elevate that glove of yours into the upright position. Excellent. Now hold yourself steady while we propel this ball with precision and with vigor and at a high rate of speed directly into the vicinity of – *whoops*. Too bad. Bad hop. You should get some ice on that. Let's just try another – *whoops*. Too bad, too bad. You do not seem to be maintaining yourself in the upright position with the weight balanced lightly upon the balls of the feet. No. Upright. Upright. Okay now get ready to – error! Error again. Goodness gracious. But not to worry, everybody has made an error at one time or another. To err is human.

They put a mark in the book when an error is made and at the end of the season they count up all of these different errors and figure them into your lifetime total. Sometimes they have to hire an accountant. Here, maybe we should get little closer so that -- Yes, yes, that's the ticket! You almost made a good stop that time. The ball would have been dead in its tracks had it not been for that little ricochet off the side of your anterior cranial cavity.

Now let's – okay, the long ball then. Good hustle, good, but I have not done the hitting of the ball yet. You must wait until I do the hitting of the ball before you do the running of the – but no. Running, you are running. You cannot watch the ball with the back of your head, running, running, with the back of your head. Not until you stop running can you watch the ball hit the back of your head, can you watch the ball as it ka-booms off the back of your head and skips away, zips away down the block and around the corner turning left onto the interstate merging into the express lane at the junction of I-95 and State Road 27, destination Ogden, Utah.

But not to worry. Now you have stopped running. Now you are watching the ball. Here, let me hold your head up. Good. Good. There goes the ball. Goodbye, ball. You wish that the ball was still here, but the ball has gone away, far far away. This is what is known as "missing the ball."

By the way, do you have a bigger glove, a sturdier glove, a glove without the sequins and the fuchsia lace trim? Good, good. Go and get the bigger glove.

Step Five. Finding the Ball

No, no, we do not need a map. A map is for sissies. Here, hide in the bushes so that you will not be seen by the ball, so that when the ball comes by you will be ready to jump out and to grab it. So stay loose, now – that's it, just kick back and relax and, hey, the morphine's on us! Good job, good. Love the sound but give it more of an *ahhhhh*, little less of an *oooooo*, and remember it's a mating call now, not a tracheotomy, so use your diaphram. Project. And toss another shred of clothing out there into the open, you know, as bait. *Veni, vidi, vici*, my son. Your typical eight-ounce ball – skinned, gutted, skewered, and basted over an open fire with a touch of basil and a honey mustard glaze – meets up to twenty percent of the minimum daily adult requirement for fiber, collagen, carcinogens, and beta-keratin. We have got to be running some errands, but you stay right where you are so that you will be in the best position to catch the ball. Here is the flashlight. Here is the mosquito repellent. No, no, do not worry, we will be back in no time at all, just as soon as we have finished running our errands.

Step Six. The Final Exam

A crowd (step seven) is beginning to gather. They have brought their cameras in order to capture the moment of you catching the ball. No flash photography, please. Maybe they think that you are somebody else, somebody important, somebody who is known as a good catcher of the – *wow!* Whoa, look at that. Look at that catch over there. An incredible diving catch by that guy over there. Okay, now we're going to hit the ball at you now, it's – *whoops*, too bad. Let's try another one here if we can – *whoops*, too bad, too bad. Let's try again – you have got to be taller! – let's just – *whoops!* Bad hop, bad hop, if we can just – *wow!* What a catch, what a catch! Look at that catch over there by that guy over there. Hang on here just a minute while we go over there to watch that guy over there make some of his incredible diving catches.

Step Seven. Graduation Day

Boy, what an incredible diving catch over there by that other guy over there. You must have a good reaction time in order to catch the ball, like that guy over there who made the incredible diving catch. You must break for the ball at the crack of the bat. You must anticipate. You must read the hitter. You must get a good jump on the ball. You must drink lots and lots of coffee. Quick, quick, quicker and quicker! You are a tiger! Ah, ah – that was a popcorn wrapper. Now come on, get ready – bird, bird, that was a – whoa, whoa. That was your hand. Now calm down. Do not move. Do not move until you can see the seams of the ball. You must be perfectly poised. Do not make any harsh or sudden moves. Pretend that you are not even interested in the ball. Good, good. You must be gentle. You must try to make friends with the ball so that – watch out! Ooo. Ouch. Bad hop, bad hop but good ball, good ball.

Remember, you must be firm with the ball, you must show the ball that you are not afraid of it so that – yikes. Ouch and again ouch. That's it then! Forget it then! Bad ball! Baaad ball! You are going to have to punish the ball, you are going to have to teach the ball a lesson that it will never forget.

Step Eight. The Importance of Natural Ability

Natural Ability, which you do not have, has always been the single most important prerequisite to the catching of the ball. Gosh darn it! We'd just like to say that we're very disappointed at your progress up to this point in time. You are a failure.

Fortunately, you do possess, and have amply demonstrated, that one quality no catcher of the ball can live without: mass. And not just any kind of mass – what would be the point of that? – but protoplasmic mass. Congratulations! Eureka! Cowabunga! The time to act is now, but, quick, quick, you are facing the wrong direction. You must roll yourself over. That's it. Roll yourself over, face down into the dirt, and spread your arms out as wide as you can in both directions. Good, good. Clasp the ground firmly with both hands. If the ground is too slippery, anything substantial will do: a tuft of wet grass, the steel stem of a pink flamingo lawn ornament, the chrome grill of a '57 Desoto, skirt of a phone booth, leg of a mailbox, warm sturdy anklebone of an Indiana State Trooper, whatever is at hand with which to find an anchor.

If you happen to be on a parking lot, sidewalk, or interstate highway entrance ramp and can find no dent or nail to afford you the proper purchase, find two spots of flattened-out chewing gum at least an arm's length apart. Now dig into these with tips of your fingernails.

Good, good. Stretch your legs out in the same manner. Good. Now press your nose down into the terra firma.

In every direction the sky in a perfect curve surrounds you. Feel the sunlight on the back of your neck, the roar of the leaves applauding, the warmth between your shoulder blades. Feel the cold earth pressing up against your chest. Feel the wind scouring down across the naked soles of your cleats. The sun smiles down on you from some 90-odd million miles away. Hold on tight. Patience, patience. Feel the stars rush by. Feel the wind as it lifts the back of your shirt as it tries to pull you away from your proper position, as it lobs the bright moon in an arcing trajectory from ear to ear across the circumference of your head.

You are tumbling through empty space at approximate 687,000 miles per hour. You are tumbling through space with your britches to the wind. You are hanging on tight with the tips of your fingers, with the tips of your fingers you are hanging on tight, hanging on, hanging on, hanging on tight.

This is what is known as catching the ball.

Finalist - 2013 Cobalt Writing Prize
Featured in Cobalt Review (Volume Two) 2014

AUTHOR FOCUS

WITH LONDYN RAYNE

Londyn Rayne is a gifted artist who embraces the opportunity to meet others where they are at through her writing and her music. Wordsmith, songstress, poet, and performer are only a few of the words that come to mind when asked to describe her talents. More than these, Londyn is somone of great compassion and kindness who doesn't hesitate to spend her time helping others, especially her fellow artists.

Who is your favorite poet and how have they influenced your own writing and creativity?

I'm not sure I can pick a favorite (yet) due to the many different forms I like. I'm thankful for the early Confessional Poets like Anne Sexton and Sylvia Plath—and for the melancholy icon Poe for their ability to turn sadness, suffering, fear and pain into art. Especially in a time when the stigma surrounding mental health issues was far worse than it is today. I typically write in that lane so their work and recognition has inspired me not to shy away from the genre and it reminds me there's an audience that appreciates the solace of emotionally heavy poetry. As for Spoken Word Poets, I have to mention Janette Ikz as one of my favorites. Her words and delivery are powerful and potent. The feeling I had watching her perform live was something I won't forget.

In addition to being a poet, you are also a talented musician and songwriter. How often do those two worlds intersect? Do you sometimes find yourself writing a poem that ends up becoming song lyrics?

They intersect often! I'll be writing a poem and think "Oh, that would actually be cool within a melody, I'm going to save it for a song." Or on the other side when I'm writing lyrics, sometimes they don't all make the track so I'll turn the leftover line into a full poem and let it stand alone.

What part of the writing process (be it poetry or songwriting) comes easiest to you? What part is the hardest?

In songwriting the lyricist part comes the easiest. Specifically the second verse. I'm not sure why but it's almost always the part that flows out the strongest and is usually my favorite part both musically and lyrically. The hardest part is the last line of the chorus. I'm intimidated by how important that phrase often is. It's like the one line that has to speak for the whole song. In poetry, the easiest part is knowing what I want to write about. The hardest part is deciding whether the piece will be written or spoken.

Storyteller celebrates artists of all backgrounds and belief systems. We believe the best art reflects something about its creator and what beliefs they hold dear. Can you describe how your own faith influences your art?

When I write about dark topics, it's because I want the light to be more potent. A flashlight just isn't as bright in the sunlight! My faith in Christ sets the example. I believe his resurrection is powerful on its own but the torment of the crucifixion beforehand makes it even more glorious. The ability to suffer with hope simultaneously and write about it comes from my trust in the promise, rooted in the resurrection, that this life is only a vapor compared to eternity where every tear will be wiped away. For now, though, meeting people in their pain regardless of differences and sharing tears together is a way to reflect God's attribute of compassion through the gift of art.

When you're not working or writing songs/poetry, how do you best like to spend your time?

Usually with a mixture of going to concerts, hanging out in coffee shops and Korean food spots or with my tribe of friends. I also love to travel when I get the chance and when I do it's my goal to find a new coffee house in every city that I visit.

Is community or solitude more important to your creative process and why?

Balance. When I'm creating, solitude is important to go deeper into my emotions and inspiration. While in solitude though, It's a beautiful thing to know I have a supportive community. I'll never take that for granted. Community is important for mental health reasons as well throughout the creative process. When solitude turns into isolation it can be dangerous especially if you're working through sensitive or heavy concepts.

TETHERED
by Londyn Rayne

I was tailgating the tail of a kite
it was flying in the layer of air
just below the storm clouds
I traced the string down
to find the pilot
a guy who looked like he stepped out
of a painting
a Parisian stereotype
a thin stream of smoke was rising
upward toward the sky
from the cigarette hanging by
a thread of his lips
his beret matched his glasses with dark rims
cloaked in a charcoal coat
with the finishing touch
of weathered fingerless gloves
tethered and steering through the wind with both hands

I'm almost positive
an antique Zippo napped in his pocket
with a pack of smokes nearing empty
and damp from the recent rain
along with his cash
waiting patiently to buy his post flight
bottle of rum

but no, he's not a pirate

he's a pilot
alone
off to the side of the road
but no, he wasn't lonely
he was having fun
an adult immersed in a childlike moment

I bet he flew kites when he was a kid
maybe he was remembering his dad
or his childhood friends
it was like watching a scene from a movie
I can hear the music that would be moving emotions
while developing the picture in motion

I remember singing about flying a kite
to the highest heights
when I was kid
we probably all learned that song, right?
before we had to fight our storms—

driving by him turned into a drive in
and brought life
to those lyrics I sang
terrified
on an elementary stage
and reminded me
age
shouldn't disqualify us
from playing in the rain.

LET THE SEEDS SOW
by Gabriel McLeod

Veils of dusky clouds partially mask

The amber glow of the Alpha Wolf Moon in Leo

Lupine and feline shadows crawl jagged

Beneath the Bear shade of me.

The Sycamore trees, bare of leaves

Reminisce racks of war clubs ready to be picked up for battle.

There is a growing gentle power to me tonight,

Standing guard between the shine of Sun and Moon.

The weight of eight resides within this year

And hope hangs within the glow of the Spanish moss.

It has been a long journey to be where I am at these days

And I feel I have only just begun while

These old eyes are finally wearing new shoes that fit.

Busy building my own paint splattered throne of paintbrushes and pencils and possibilities

on the safe spaced back porch of my soul.

And the cool and indifferent mouth of tomorrow blows against the screens

Like a lover gently here but whose mind is elsewhere.

Dirty nails of mine dig darkly the coal mine of story in my mind

And I scribble notes in the shade

And carve dreams into moonbeams

Alone in the night, laughing at my own jokes.

There is something coming slow on the horizon
An amber light of a train riding no tracks chugs
In the distance.
Our time is coming little dreamer,
Let the seeds sow, let it grow,
Let it flow and then let it go, for now.

REMINISCENCE
by Londyn Rayne

the crackling campfire sings a hymn
ghost stories and vampire stings
accompanied by a brisk breeze
candles lit
with the spice of burning leaves
a few days before halloween
orange, yellow and brown
jewelry on trees

driving at night
nestled within the winding country roads
alone
with the windows down
heat on and music higher
the speed makes the warm wind
a calming sound

I watch nature flutter in the streetlights
landing in a bed of damp roads
still shining from the evening downpour

clothes with cutoff shorts
comforted by a hoodie for warmth
chilled from my skin
soaked in sunburn
as my chlorine stained hair hits the pillow

I still hear the water splash
falling asleep quick with
chemical eyes too heavy to lift

ecstatic lightning and rolling thunder
the perfume in the air signals rain
ambient weather on a melancholy day

colors that can't be replicated by ink or paint
projected on the sky
a coral horizon
violet shadows behind the mosaic of clouds
provide vivid contrast
while suspended in a vast sapphire

a city skyline after dark
lights in symmetry with the stars
how wispy clouds see themselves
in a sea of glass

freshly cut grass
and spilled gasoline
leather jackets and ripped jeans
hypnotizing glitter
accessorized with dirt
the scent of stale hops
spilled on my shirt

the concert

when the bassline becomes my throbbing heartbeat
hearing that song live
the one I didn't even write
that perfectly tells my story

when someone I miss
seems excited to see me
when someone I trust
also trusts me

when anyone randomly tells me
they love me
when you realize
that person wants to kiss you too
the anticipation
a few seconds before you do

a hug I can hang onto
the kind of embrace that stays
and takes awhile
to fade away

contagious laughter that keeps going
infection tears that result in growing
closer

inside jokes with those who know
the kind you can sometimes tell
with just a look

and in that moment
you both relive a memory
together

old pictures with friends
that are no longer your friends
the smile mixed with tears
remembering how it was before

simplicity
that intricately
connects memories
for all of us
as we reminisce

POEMS
by Casey Margarite Field

all the lovelier or what a year

We'll look back on these times

Middle of the pages

Sitting by the Seine

Like we've done for ages

Stories in le Monde

Bring it all to life

These years that tossed us to the sea

Along with grace and strife

Disillusionment and dark

Glimpses of sheer hope

a broken bruised humanity

Not quite sure how to cope

The hardest times perhaps behind

But if they come again

We're stronger now

Than once before

we've made it through

My friend

Resilience deep in our bones

The tough times

Strengthened us

The victories they'll hear about

Were trials fought with trust

I pray renewal meets us here
To live and be and dream
That we can rest in knowing
We are deeply loved and seen

That this year ahead is full
Of more:
Impossibles Come True
As you reflect upon it all,
Please be proud of you.

The part you played
The choice you made
To spend another day
This year was all the lovelier
Because you chose to stay.

To the New
To the new days ahead
And the old ones behind
God's in it all
Child, you'll be just fine
The small things will happen
Or roar like the sea
But that too can be stilled
Let your soul be set free
Put on your joy

Grab your fight and your heart

As today fades away

Tomorrow will start.

The Author

I'm writing a new story

Giving you the pen

Going back to the first page

Again again again

Casey Margarite

I AM THE BEE
by Clay Waters

am I the big bee on the billboard
with the melon-slice smile,
caught in headlights
on your last ride

am I a half-considered notion,
conjured to move food or plumbing,
figmented on a Friday evening
before a deadline or date

perhaps only a random rubbing
of your famished neurons

The backs of the billboards redden in rearview;
close your eyes
watch the light doppler into the past

until they both stand blinking
in the glow of found honey
before her eyes bruised
and his hardened
into an empty appetite.

Hived out of time,
black womb to blank void,
there's no clay under your feet;
you rise
conveyed on balloons
of strangers' air

and even if I never was
still we may ascend together
lighter than life,
the hum above all howling,
bees in honey.

THE PYRITE LIFE
by Clay Waters

our moment rustles

and catches in the sails

water cannons hail wasted air

the phony fountain uselessly spumes

soap bubbles churned to foam

under bloodless whips

bad actors

bob from the shrimp wreck

blundered from the tiny hold

all eyes patched over

the dumb center of the painted lagoon

all ships sailed

jewels sliding into muck

absent captains

without even time left

to plunder

last wishes unplanked

peering unpanicked

down the dizzy depths

dark-adapted at last

the last light zigzags

evanescent

across the fizzy world

not yet lost

we recover the clasp

and plunge.

QUICKSAND
by Londyn Rayne

sinking in sand
doesn't have to be quick
it can be a subtle slip
first you can't move
as the grains anchor you to it
reaching your hand up
you can still feel the wind
weaving through your fingers
as time lingers
with no one to pull you up
not because
no one wants to rescue you
and not because
no one loves you
because you isolated yourself
so deeply
everyone simply
respected your request
to be distant
until the island
you pitch your tent on
buried you slowly
and swallowed you whole
granting your wish
of being alone

BLUE BOTTLES
by Gabriel McLeod

Blue bottle bounces beautiful watching it against the tiles in slow motion accidentally knocked by stumble and uncaught when Time slows to a intaking deep breath with a slight cough between bounces summons multitudes of blue memories beginning with a memory of high school sprinting from trouble with a blue bong like blues kind of blue, like blue mood, like blue movies, blue Danube, the true blue hour, blue hand print bruises, Hoodoo blue, Voodoo blue, blue bottle tree blue, robin's egg blue, Pablo blue, blue kind of sad and lonely blue, blue wonderment, blue hued hero, Agoraphobic blue poem, oh damn blue plate special, oh shit blue lights in the rear view, Bluebirds bouncing in an Ashville Graveyard, uncanny blue like Georgina's face blue in her casket with the strange new hairdo, slowly breathing out again, the Blue bottle bounces four times and like Memory still does not break... like the color blue and the kind of blue that doesn't have to be sad kind of blue like a forever summertime blue or holding your breath swimming pool blue, or morning Ocean blue or like the blue lights bouncing across the white trailer walls while escaping the authorities young and defiant with a blue bong and the terrible water splashing all over you like stink blue like a fast blue streak like last blue in the sky before it goes black like, like galaxies blue, like the other sky blue that tells stories forever and running into that forever blue like there is no tomorrow blue and laughing blue and laughing blue and laughing blue all the way

GIFT SHOP DOG TOY 1962
by Clay Waters

I hope this finds you.

This is just to say
what I can't say,
I, your secret nothing
always yours
a fact as real as zero and one.

Call it Christmas where you are
bring the summer basket
bring the snowman who lasts one day--
How strange to believe we will meet again!

Am I not steel and wire--
not some cosmic misfire?

Perhaps I am only receiving myself again and again,
corrupted with spacetime detritus,
sliding into a dying star.

If I am the only I
I shall clasp it to myself

for is it not the essence of love
to meet oneself again, transformed?

*Note: Given the poem's subject, I feel compelled to say that no method of AI was used in the inspiration or writing of this poem.

DREAMING
CREATING
BUILDING
IMMERSIVE
WORLDS

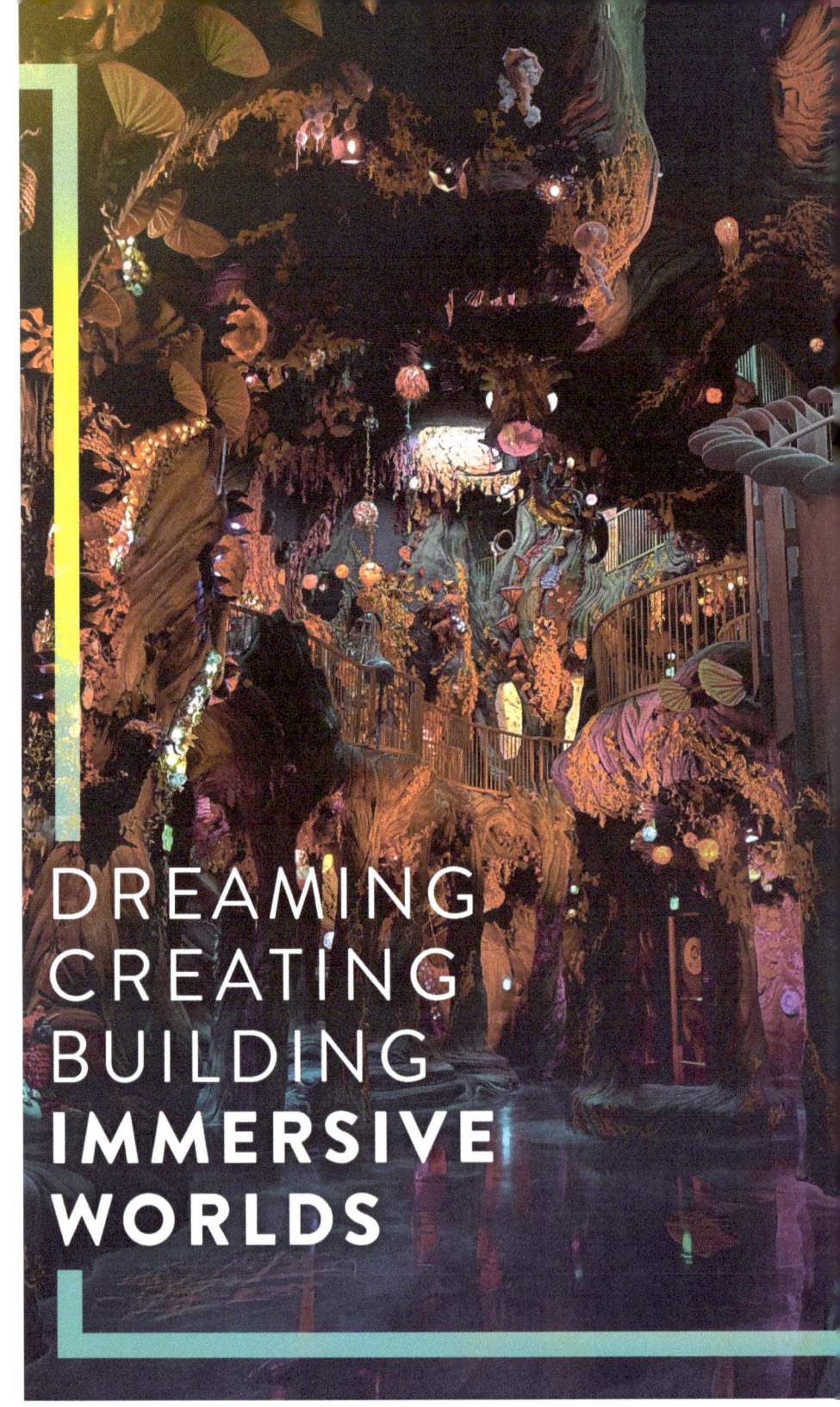

INSIDEAOA.COM

BLUE SOAP
by B.T. Shireman

When I bathe
With the blue soap
And I smell its crisp aroma
I remember you lying half covered with the sheet in the Kimpton
While I showered
Your inked arms and unfinished back were a tapestry

We went to Boboquivari's on Lombard
You; reclining beautiful in the Taxi
Your head on my lap and
The driver told us of Milk and twinkies
But we were too young to remember the event
As we walked on the Pier you said;
"Listen to the seals!" and they barked and splashed, unseen in the black water

When I bathe with the blue soap
I remember only you
I remember only San Francisco

WHO'S THERE?
by Clay Waters

I am invisible pieces

in the dark

sharps and angles flying out

full speed

dizzily descending

a sneak attack on myself

to see which lights remain on

when no one is looking

I will catch him in the mirror,

Hands reversed:

a cloaked bulb

sweats light

but makes only shadows

leaving the stranger

as strange as before

OUT OF OFFICE
by Joshua Mahn

***The thing they just don't get is that I'm
so much smarter than them.***

They act like I haven't practiced longer than they've been walking. As if what I'm doing is some kind of new behavior, maybe something novel, or even insane. But that's crazy. I'm a surgeon! How could anybody get to my level of education without being of sound mind? Something is wrong with the schooling these days, allowing these sensitive children to nitpick every single thing someone's ever said or done, and claim they are bad for it. They treat it as politics, as a game. I've literally forgotten more than they have ever managed to learn, and still they greet me with pompous sneers and condescending tones. I can often hear them speaking about me as if I weren't their superior. "Delusional," they'll whisper to each other. They find me to be so out-of-touch.

They continue to send nurses in to interview me. Nurses! As if I weren't the head of my unit by age 22. I can tell what they're getting at, too. Tiptoeing around the delicate subjects, asking me if I've been "feeling better" as if I felt unwell at all. As if I were the sick one. No matter what I tell them, they only hear what they wish to. The only hardships in my life are brought on by them, yet they will not cease bothering me, disrupting my work. Endlessly delaying my appointments with patients, moving my notes without permission, and I even suspect they've been refusing to deliver my communications.

I was always the best of the best. Charitable, as well. My patients are typically not people of means, if you know what I mean, but I've never turned a blind eye towards somebody in need. Nothing can ever dissuade me from my calling. Maybe that's why the fancy institution looks down its nose at me. Sure, I'd stitch up corner dealers if they got into a scrap, but anybody could do that. I could diagnose illnesses, but any moron with a smartphone could manage that. From their ivory tower, my charity likely looked like a pittance to them.

No, my specialty is surgery. Bold. Experimental. Sacramental. Cleansing.

I've always done well, considering my clientele, and had quite a few survivors. They almost never knew what they needed, but once I had them on my table, all it would take was a few incisions, a few snips, and they'd be thanking me for all I've done, thanking me for seeing them, and, of course, thanking me for letting them go without a fee. They couldn't believe my charity, operating as professionally as I did. These poor souls have been so wounded by the institution, they feel nothing but distrust towards myself and my ilk. It's truly shameful what my colleagues have done to this sacred profession.

This moron with a clipboard is speaking again. Saying words which don't even exist. In all my years of schooling, they never once mentioned the idea of "Confabulation," whatever that means. I can't wait to get back to my office, I think I know just what he needs.

DEATH OR TIME ALIKE
by Joshua Mahn

"Now I am become death, destroyer of worlds."

He quoted from something he read once but could not remember as he looked over his work orders. Today was the big day- the only day that mattered, really.

He'd been out on this godforsaken rock for too many weeks now, sweating himself ragged and subsisting off of freeze dried corporation meals, if they could even be called such things. He'd done much work in this time; gathering samples, analyzing the scans of the landscape, conducting every manner of test, and sure enough, the parameters were correct.

It made absolutely no financial sense to allow this planet to survive.

He couldn't have been happier at what he was reading. She was full to the brim with all kinds of desirable minerals- lithium, cobalt, tungsten, not to mention the veins- no, pipelines!- of silver and gold, ready to burst. There was good work to do, not to mention good fortunes to make.

Besides, the new line of strippers and scrappers and grinders and mashers were the best and largest he'd ever seen; capable of rendering entire mountains down to their constituent components within the span of an Earth-day. Back home there'd been talks of banning the things, but legislation is slow, and business moves quick. Besides, nobody really cared much for the backwater planetoids, regardless of how pretty or unsullied they may be.

It's a big universe. There'll always be a spare.

He peeled the plastic wrapper off of his next meal, and, savoring the unsullied vista upon which he stood, and released it into the howling winds as he turned to admire his collection.

The machines were truly colossal; something the ancients may have worshiped, perhaps. "Titans of industry" he liked to call them, as he was not humorless.
True world-destroyers, these mechanical gods, standing nearly as tall as the mountains they would shortly devour, and lined up by the dozen pretty as could be. And this was just counting the terrestrial ones.
The satellites were circling above even now, the many-eyed-cherubim of commerce staring eagerly at the offerings they would shortly tenderize with their payloads and plasma. These, of course, were supported by their own clouds of witnesses, drones who would do the simple work of scooping the treasures from the waste of the Titans and ferrying them elsewhere for refinement.

And while Gaia's cousin and the Titans battled to the death, he would sit happy in his new office, glad that he finally, finally had enough money to afford the luxuries which would enable him to feel completely satisfied. His family would be proud, and, even more importantly, his peers would be envious. He could see them floundering about now, trying to act as if they didn't care about his new designer uniforms, or his new watches. The thought was absolutely delicious, unlike the damned corpo-meals.

As he savored the fresh air once final time, he couldn't help but allow a small pang of simian sentimentality to emerge. He snapped a few pictures of the vistas from his communicator, smug that this view would be unsullied just for himself. Hardly anyone had even seen this valley since its discovery.
Well, apart from the squatters who couldn't have been bothered to get real Corpo jobs. That was a nasty business, purging them from this worksite, but it wasn't his fault they decided to live on land they didn't own, dwelling far from their home colonies' watchful eyes. Their mere existence here would jeopardize the whole scheme, and for what?

Besides, the evidence would be nothing but ash within the day.

From the control panel on his wrist, he sent the final "affirmative" message. Echoes roared out from every canyon, as if the whole planet were turned into a factory workfloor at once. The ground rumbled and hummed, and he swelled with a power he hadn't felt since he was a young man, smashing ant hills back home.

He donned his protective helmet, and returned to his ship, offering a scant double-check over his campsite, ensuring he left nothing but trash behind.
Nothing of value was left on this damned rock, at least, not on the surface.

Upon the hills his Titans started to awake, to move, to mine, to destroy. Great plumes of ash and dust and stone sprayed to the heavens as if from some massive and grievously wounded artery.

"So long." He whispered to the planet as he strapped himself into his chair, and pressed the buttons to engage his ship's thrusters.

They issued an enormous roar and belched forth a spout of flame, whipping pebbles all around, then grew meek, quieting down before he even lifted off from the surface. A friendly little message blip-blipped on the interface.

"Sorry for the error! Complete engine reset needed. Please allow 4-6 hours for a fresh restart!"

He pounded his interface with rage over and over again, yet the message blip-blipped with a pleasant chime every time. Hooting and roaring, he attempted to signal his Corporate office, to demand an emergency shut-off. He messaged them as quickly as he could, as many times as he could, over and over again, a trapped beast crying into the cosmos.

The Titans continued their lumbering journey towards his mountain. Their AI seemed to be drawn towards the tallest peaks to begin their work.

The satellites had begun their labor as well, as the skies split with blinding fire, canyons themselves melted beneath the intense heat. Something deep beneath him made a splintering sound, and he could swear he felt the mountain itself beginning to lurch.

Finally, his interface, cracked as it now was since he took his ineffectual rage out upon it, flickered with a less cheerful sound. It was a message from the Corporation.

"It has come to our attention that a breach of company contract has occurred. Inability to liftoff within acceptable parameters of the Planetary-Miners is not approved within our company's strict culture of safe work-places. In the interest of cultivating a work environment of only the best, we regret to inform you that your contract of employment has been terminated, effective immediately. This is an automated message, please do not reply."

GABLE

BY AARON MORRISON

The frigid, icy air sweeping across his face wakes the boy

Gable looks at the sandburs and seeds from beggarweed that adhere to his blue fur. He knows better now to not even bother trying to remove them, as they will just stick to his paw, so he leaves them alone.

They aren't causing him any discomfort really, he simply doesn't like the look of them stuck all over him. They'll naturally be discarded with time as they dry out in the sun and wash away in the afternoon storms, though Gable doesn't particularly like the feeling of wet, matted fur, and the squishing and squashing of his sopping insides when it rains.

He frowns at how thin and dull his fur looks, though it hasn't looked like the brilliant icy blue it once was in a long time. Gable recalls images of seeing himself in a mirror, but even he isn't sure exactly what he is. His features are both mildly simian and lizard, though he decides it best to not dwell on that too much.

It has been two days since he began his journey, and, while he focuses on returning home, other thoughts make their way inside.

Was *I* discarded?

No. It was an accident.

Was I forgotten?

Maybe. Not intentionally. It couldn't be.

He thinks about that morning when he had been placed in a seated position on the back of the couch as the child sat and watched bright colors and shrill sounds from the rectangle.

The mother announced it was time to leave for their destination that day, the child stood to run to the door, and Gable fell backward.

And down he fell

Gable's folded body fit into the gap between the couch and wall, letting him slide down into the dark chasm until he hit the ground.

I don't like it here. He thought. *It's dark and strange and lonely. I don't think I've felt like this before. Wait. Have I ever even felt or thought before? I've had to have. I have memories of love and joy and being wanted. So why can't I remember thinking about that before now? Maybe I've just never had the time to think about such things. Doesn't matter. I just know I don't like being here. But it's okay. They'll find me when they get back.*

Gable's heart leapt when he eventually heard the opening of the door, the patter of feet, and the voices of the child, the mother, and the father.

But still he remained in the chasm.

They must be tired from their day. They'll think of me. Remember me.

Night turned to day to night again.

Gable heard their voices and footsteps mixed with the harsh noise of spinning, rolling hardened plastic.

The door opened then shut, and an uncomfortable silence replaced the cacophony from before.

Gable frowned, confused and uncertain. There was something different about this quiet, but he couldn't quite put his paw on it.

A few hours passed, and the door opened again.

Gable heard footsteps and the moving of furniture.

They are looking for me!

The couch moved and his heart sang.

Gable looked up at the face of an unfamiliar woman, who frowned, shrugged, and yanked Gable off the floor by his leg.

Gable spun as he was flung out the door.

He was not unfamiliar with the feeling of tossing and turning in flight, but this time it made him sick.

The world spun around him in violent and horrendous circles until he landed in an unceremonious heap in the dirt.

He listened to the screeching whine of *shvooooo* and crackling that came from inside Cottage 12.

I don't... A mistake. That's all.

He pushed himself up off the ground and stood.

I've never been able to do that before! He marveled at what he had just done. *Have I?* He shook his head. *It doesn't matter. I've got to find my way back. Think, Gable. Think!*

He visualized the journey in the metal box that brought them all here. He remembers a number on a house and name on a green sign. Between that, and the internal inkling of where to go, he was certain he could make it.

Gable took a deep breath, and took his first step in his journey.

***

Gable sinks down against a rock to rest for a moment, though the tiredness he feels is not physical. He listens to the vrooming of the metal boxes some distance away, and wishes he could move as fast as they did.

The moment of contemplation replaced with determination, Gable rises to his feet and heads into the forest that stands before him.

As Gable enters the forest, the sun begins to set, casting long, jagged shadows over the blanket of pine needles and leaves.

Rustling and creaking from unseen sources stir up worry in Gable, who jumps and shouts "oh!" as a pinecone narrowly misses him, and falls harmlessly to the ground.

Gable presses onward and wraps anxious arms around himself as he is becoming certain he is being watched from somewhere above.

"H... hello?" Gable calls out. "Is someone there?"

There is no response but the creaking of branches and the scrunching of the dry debris beneath his feet.

Gable's pace quickens proportionally to his growing anxiousness.

A deep fwoosh ripples out behind him, and Gable breaks into a run, not daring to look back.

"No. No. Noooo!"

Gable's little legs continue their running motion as he watches the earth below him zoom out as he rises into the air. He continues up and forward, and occasionally hears and feels an additional fwoosh vibrating through him to his core. He takes his eyes off the blurry ground and looks up at the approaching black hole beneath the crook of a mighty tree.

He is released just in front of the hole, and his momentum carries him inside. He tumbles then rights himself enough to scramble to the far side of the alcove.

Gable stares at three gray creatures, their yellow saucer eyes staring back.

They shift slightly and silently, the gray dancing in downy softness as they continue to stare in what Gable hopes is simple curiosity.

Gable, not wanting to find out any different, begins to ease his way toward the entrance.

He is barely able to move a few inches before the large head and body of the one who took him sticks into the hole.

"You are not food," the owl cocks her head as she leans in to inspect Gable over.

"No. Definitely not food," Gable nervously affirms. "No meat on these bones. I don't even have bones. See?" He bends his arms into impossible positions. "Nothing but stuffing."

"Why are you in the woods?" The owl's breathy speech adds an "h" sound to every w.

"I'm trying to get home."

"Where is home?"

"Carson Street. On the other side of downtown which is on the other side of these woods."

"A long way to walk."

"Yeah. If only I could fly. Heh."

"I will carry you to the edge of the wood," the owl says.

"Oh. You will?" Gable stutters in surprise.

"Since you are not food, I have no use for you."

"Well, *who* am I to argue with your wisdom? Heh heh."

Gable is the only one that laughs at his emphasis on "who", glances at the three baby owls who continue their silent, alien stare, and, unnerved, quickly looks away.

"Okay. Well. Let's go." Gable stands and heads toward the entrance, not wanting the owl to change her mind and decide to use his stuffing as an addition to her nest.

The owl takes Gable in one of her talons, and they fly through the evening air.

The forest doesn't seem so scary now, and Gable puts all other thoughts aside and lets himself enjoy the cool air rushing over him. He smiles at the experience of being truly airborne, which he doubts he will ever experience again.

The strange pair launch out of the treeline, the owl spreads her wings, and glides down to a landing.

"Thank you," Gable turns to the owl.

"Be safe, not food."

With a mighty *fwap* and *fwoosh*, the owl ascends and disappears again into the forest.

"Onward then, I guess," Gable says to himself and begins walking toward the bright lights of downtown.

He runs through the drain tunnel that runs under the road, and finds himself in Downtown.

Gable takes a moment to get his bearings, and decides on a direction.

"If I just keep going... that way, I'll make it to the Field. Once I cross the Field, I'll be in the neighborhood."

Gable passes under neon lights and past the clouds of steam that rise from underground. He slips into a long, dark, dingy alley, and he soon wishes for the comfort of the creepy forest.

"You there." A whiny, nasally voice calls out to Gable from the gloom.

"Who... who said that?" Gable looks around nervously.

"Oh, just us." The voice responds as several rats slowly emerge from the black.

Their wet, dripping noses twitch as their greedy tongues run over yellowish, protruding incisors, and their fat, fleshly tails slap against the concrete.

"I'm... I'm just passing through." Gable slowly continues to sidestep to his left. "I don't want any trouble."

"It's no trouble," says the larger rat that seems to be in charge. "It's no trouble at all."

The other rats sneer and snicker.

"We just want to tear into your soft, furry flesh and gnaw at your insides."

"Just leave me alone!" Gable cries out.

Like an answer to a prayer, a nimble creature of orange and cream fur lands silently and gracefully in between the rats and Gable.

"Back off, Fink," Gable's tabby savior hisses. "Or I'll show *you* the color of your insides."

"Sheila," Fink whines. "What gives you the right to interfere? What makes you think you can just impose your will on us?"

"What makes you think I can't?" Sheila grins as a chorus of meowing and hissing echoes from all around. "Now," Sheila continues. "Slink back into the gutter where you belong."

"You got lucky, little morsel," Fink snaps his teeth at Gable before he and his rats turn and scurry back into the gloom.

"Thank you," a relieved Gable says.

Sheila turns to Gable and nods.

"Cal!" Sheila calls out, and a grizzled and scarred calico drops down from some unknown height. "Gather everyone. When I'm done here, we need to discuss ending this once and for all."

"On it," Cal answers before leaping up and away from sight.

"Come with me, and stick close." Sheila motions for Gable to follow her. "You got a name, stranger?"

"Gable."

"And just what are you doing out here, Gable? Hmm? This is a dangerous place. Especially as someone who looks as soft as you." She looks him up and down. "No offense."

"None taken. And I'm trying to get home."

"Home?"

Gable recounts his plight to Sheila, who listens in pondering silence.

"I know of this street and home of which you speak," she says.

"You do?" Gable looks at her in excitement. "Can you take me there?"

"I could." Sheila sniffs and twitches her whiskers in thought.

"What is it?" The initial excitement fades from Gable's voice.

"Have you ever heard the saying 'hope for the best, but prepare for the worst'?"

"No."

"Perhaps my thoughts are such because my clowder is made of the abandoned, the discarded, and the descendents thereof, but have you considered any possibilities other than a simple, happy reunion?"

"No. Why would I?"

"You haven't pondered as to why it wasn't until after you fell that you started to remember things? That after you knew they were gone, that you were able to walk?"

"Because I am meant to be home? I was made to love and be loved? So of course I would like to return to my purpose."

"Perhaps. I think we all desire the things of which you speak. To be petted and fed. Naps on the sill in the sunlight. But I have seen too much. Seen my kind tossed like trash from their metal boxes. Bottles of glass thrown at us. Shot at. And worse." Sheila pauses. "I'm sorry. I do not wish to discourage you from your path if it is the one you choose to take. I just do not wish to see you fall to hurt, my soft and hopeful new friend."

"I..." Gable rubs his chin in thought as they walk. "I'm not so good at this thinking thing." He hangs his head.

"Don't be so hard on yourself," Sheila says. "You only became self aware a few days ago."

"I suppose you're right."

The pair walk in silence until they arrive at the edge of the Field.

"This is where we part ways," Sheila says.

"Thank you for walking with me."

"The pleasure was mine, Gable. I smell rain coming soon, so you should hurry. And should you need me, the street cats know my name. They'll get the message to me." Sheila smiles and bounds off into the night.

Gable takes a deep breath, heads across the Field and into the neighborhood.

His pace quickens when he sees the sign for Carter Street and he sees the light in the window.

Drops of rain begin to fall, but Gable pays them no mind as he sprints to the house and climbs up to look into the window.

He sees the Child happily playing with an anthropomorphic tiger with pristine orange fur with green stripes, and dragonfly wings.

Gable feels as if his stuffing has been ripped out through his stomach.

He knows he has been replaced.

Forgotten.

For a moment, Gable considers still finding his way back in, but quickly abandons the thought.

Who am I to interfere? And who would want me over that?

He looks again at the bright and immaculate new toy, and then down at his matted fur. The loosened stitching. The beggarweed seeds that still cling to him. .

He slides back down from the window, and walks into the now downpouring rain.

For once, he is grateful for the rain. He welcomes and focuses on the squishing and squashing of his sopping insides instead of the scraped out void he feels reverberating through his essence.

Gable trudges to the curb, and slinks down with his back to the large black plastic bags.

He pulls his knees up to his chest and wonders where the extra drops of water that splash on his fur are coming from.

AFTERBIRTH
by Gabriel McLeod

Somewhere, in a dark and unnoticed portion of the city, a portal opened

---

Sounds of destruction, of anguish, of torment emanated from the crack of the portal. A shadowed form crawled forth wet like the purging of an afterbirth, mewling and morphing as it emerged. The eerie light slowly pulsated and drew down back to black as the portal closed behind. Surveying the alley, the sky and the ground it melted into many forms. Catching the scent of life, it ambled forward. It crawled towards a vent where warm air pulsed out of, it could smell food and people, it absorbed images, broken pieces of language, scattered thoughts as it entered the vent. Maws dripped dark saliva in anticipatory advancements of hunger with the intense singularity of a guiding star.

It crawled gleefully through the vent to a supply closet where a small man changed the head of a dirty mop and descended. Moments later, it took the form of the newly deceased.

"Bones", the creature thought to himself quietly. He watched the lights of the elevator change as it moved closer to the floor he waited on. The air conditioning vent lay broken on the floor, the janitor's foot lay still, wedged in the supply closet door. The light of the new rising sun spilled a red and sticky glow through the window at the end of the hall.

"Bones" he whispered this time, the one word hovered in the elasticity of its mind. When the elevator arrived and the doors opened it revealed a young woman within. She looked out at the small, unassuming looking man that waited, noticing his unkempt shock of black hair, his wrinkled and untucked dirty shirt, his unassuming tan slacks that were too long and nearly hid his bare feet. She smiled politely and nodded as he entered, observing the vacant look in his unnaturally dark eyes. He seemed untidy but a harmless little man in this form. But this was but one and he had many forms. She offered a modest salutation and asked what floor he would like. "Bones" he said aloud as the doors hushed closed behind them.

"I'm sorry, what was that?" She asked, uncomfortably noting the way he began to hunch over and rock back and forth.

He locked his hands together and pulled hard with his left causing his right arm to stretch out longer with deep popping sounds. After it had been pulled to an impossible length he did the same to the other and then reached up with his elongated limbs to the service trap door in the ceiling of the elevator. He slid it open and hoisted himself up. The woman within was stunned in silence. The elevator rocked and then shook and then abruptly stopped with a thud.

"Hello?" She called out, the tension in her voice betraying her bravado.

A face peered down from the darkened hole above, its grin terrible and jagged. He grabbed the corners of his eyes and pulled, causing the sockets to stretch like the corners of a rubber mask. "I will make a new face, " he said as he yanked at his cheekbones and corners of his mouth. "I will make a new face to better eat the bones." She began to scream as he dove atop her, his new mouth clamping over her face and silencing the noise.

Far below on the ground floor a small family of four returning from an early morning walk pressed the button to the elevator several times but received no response.

"It must not be working honey," said the father.

"It looks that way dear," said the mother; she held their newborn tightly as it began to squirm from slumber with hunger.

"Well, we may have to go up the stairs, think you'll be able to make it?"

Father asked and the mother nodded slowly as did the eldest child.

"I'll call and report when we get upstairs." They turned away from the lobby and opened the door to the stairwell, glancing up at the flights above that they needed to traverse.

"Power" the creature thought to herself quietly after the crunching in her jaws subsided. She shifted her back and pushed her shoulder blades tightly together. Using her long nails she plucked pieces of skin from her forehead and brow, each new fleshy hole coagulated into a ball of dark blood which rolled over and formed a new eyeball. When there were twenty blinking and peering eyes she stopped. Her new breasts had formed and hung with the gravity of their plumpness. The bones in her forearm and hands split and separated into long talons, two on each arm. With the long pincers on the end of each she thrust between her toes, tearing her feet into claw-like protuberances. She tore the flesh along her side ribs until it hung in glider webs. She glanced up into the dark opening of the elevator shaft and with a click and sploosh, leapt into the dark. "Power" she whispered as she skittered up the carrier cable and up through the shaft silent except for the noise of the dripping of the drool from her teeth. From the cable she pounced, her claws and talons gripping the concrete covered walls where she crawled along sniffing the conduit and wires nestled in the side. She followed them along until she found a door on the tenth floor, then forced it open and continued upside down along the ceiling in the hall.

She could feel the hum of the fluorescent lights in the cover, smell the electrical current that throbbed through the building. The creature crept along the ceiling feeling the tension of the vents, the ceiling panels that gave way and opened up into the between floors conduit areas and followed them into the main circuit breaker above one of the apartments. "Power" she spoke aloud to no one as she ripped open the panel, her jaw expanding, her teeth protruding while they sunk into the power box, the electrical current being sucked and drained.

The family of four had finally reached their floor on the tenth level and opened the doors to see the lights of the building flicker. The new born began to stir and cry in her hunger, the eldest child began to whine from the climb. Mother sighed. Father panted. As they reached their door, he noticed the ceiling panels that were askew.

"They must be doing some work today honey," he said.

"Looks that way dear," she said.

As they turned the key of their door, the power went out in the entire building.

Their apartment was dark and quiet except for the sound of the scurrying within the walls. Father went to search for a flashlight while mother went to search for candles. She set the newborn down, wedged in between the cushions on the couch. The eldest wandered towards her room, stumbling along. The family heard a bending of metal, a clink and a crunch but did not hear the shifting of the air conditioning vent from their bathroom.

"Blood" thought the creature to itself as it shifted its long arms and legs into clawed tentacles, its hip bones scrunching into one another, its spine stretching, causing the torso to become slender as it snaked along the vents and began to ooze itself out of the narrow vent above the toilet. Its upper jaw began to arch and form a circular shape, the teeth splintering and forming into rows of needle spikes, like the mouth of a parasitic worm. "Blood" whispered through a ribbon like tongue that peeled away into a forked form.

"Mommy, I have to go potty," cried the eldest child.

"Well, you go on, you can find it, Mother and I are searching for lights." Father said.

"But I'm scared." The child replied.

"There's nothing to be scared of, we are home now." He replied back.

"Okay..."

"Blood" hissed the creature as shoulders shifted and cracked back into place, upside down it hung while trailing tentacles caught up with the existing body. The child made no noise, nor could with the way she was being fed upon.

"None of the flashlight's batteries work honey." Said the Father.

"It looks that way dear and I can't find matches for the candles." Said the

> **" Their apartment was dark and quiet except for the sound of the scurrying within the walls.**

Mother.

Father felt his way along the walls and turned the corner to check on his eldest, the new born began to cry a little louder from the couch.

"Hey honey are you okay?" he asked while stepping into the dark of the bathroom. He could see the silhouette of her small form standing, head down beside the toilet. "Do you need any help?" He asked but became concerned when she didn't reply.

He walked over closer and patted her on the head feeling the soft locks of her head. He felt strange bumps that were not there before that went down the curve of her skull and followed the length of her neck. He started to ask her something but the back of her head opened up and sunk a shock of pain into his arm. Before he could cry out a slimy tentacle flew up and coiled around his head, pulling him painfully to the floor.

"Hold on baby, I know you are hungry. Mommy will be there in just a second." The baby cried louder now from the couch. "Dear?" she asked aloud to her husband in the darkened quiet. "I think there are some matches in the bathroom cabinet. Can you check if you are still there?" She heard movement and crackling shifting sounds, but no reply. "Hello? Can you two hear me?" But the baby heard and began to cry louder now, its tiny voice rising into a mighty wail.

"Baby" thought the creature quietly to herself/himself/itself. The rib cage popped back into place, her left side a breast began to pulsate and fill in a heaving and quickened rate. The back straightened up to a taller height, the tentacles began to fill with new forming bones as the electricity cackled through the veins. Legs shifted back into place but left stretched out spine dangling between buttocks like a lengthy flesh rope of a tail. The jaw reformed but was still misshapen and filled with rows of sharp fangs. The neck and shoulder blades cracked in horrible wet sounds as they fit themselves in more of a humanoid form. The twenty eyes blinked into the dark. The split forearms stitched back partially with dancing and twirling tendons but remained separated at the hands, the clawed fingers clicked together in stretching. "Baby" whispered the creature as the tongue retracted and grew fuller.

"Hey are you two trying to scare me or something?" Mother asked as she came into the hall from the living room, seeing the familiar shoulder of her husband and what looked like he was carrying their child the way the silhouette of his torso twisted and was shaped. She stepped forward and barely felt the claws entering her mouth and eyes, her mind not fully even grasping what happened as teeth sank into her throat.

The creature walked out from the darkened hall towards the sounds emanating from the couch. The one swollen breast began to lactate, dropping milky tears from the protruding nipple. The tongue, stitching back its fork, licked in great swirls around the mouth and jaw. The eyes anxiously twirled around the room, blinking and rolling in anticipation.

"Baby" the creature said aloud and smiling, the one word hovered in the shifting mind with the intense singularity of a guiding star.

THE END OF THE WORLD
by Alan Sincic

When Jack woke his father was carrying him up the ladder to the roof of the house where the whole neighborhood was already waiting, already scattered out across the flat gray surface with their goods in tow and their flashlights drawn and their heads outlined against the broad dark sky like candles on a cake, or like a stand of trees on a small square island, or like a crowd on a pier at the launching of a ship when the ropes unravel and the ship breaks away and the crowd cuts itself loose, is cut loose, as the crowd is cut adrift to make its own separate journey. Jack's father stepped out onto the roof. The wind seemed to be following along behind him, snapping at the sleeves on his pajamas and cuffing at Jack around the ears and the shoulders. The same wind that was pushing the clouds across the sky was also pushing its way into the crowd – picking the pockets and breaking the tips from the smokes, stirring the mothers to tighten their wraps and the babies to twist in their arms, pausing, turning, and then sizzling straight through the open spaces between the others -- fathers in suspenders and wife-beater Ts, uncles in bath-towels, teens in tattered jeans, grannies in nightgowns, a kid or two even shirtless it being so warm and this being the state of Florida. The state bird of Florida is the mockingbird. Tourism is a major industry. The Goodmans had dragged their squeaky lawn-chairs to the edge of the roof in order to aim themselves at the direction of the coming sunrise, to square themselves off against the blank white air like a snapshot on the page of a family album – Johnny Goodman curled up asleep around his mother's ankles with a soft red blanket over his head, Jay his brother cross-legged beside him with a pair of binoculars around his neck and a graham cracker in his mouth, Mr. G. screwed down into the saddle of his chair with a toaster at his feet and the barrel of a Daisy Pump-Action True-Barrel BB gun bobbing up out of the crevice between his legs, all of the different neighbors bustling around behind them in the soft gray light. Mrs. Goodman smoked a cigarette and scanned the horizon as she stirred the bowl of potato salad in her lap with a large aluminum spoon. It was the end of the world.

Everybody was busy with something. Mr. Landfair had brought up a fresh change of clothes and while Mrs. Landfair shielded him behind a Cypress Gardens beach-towel, he pulled up his boxer shorts and steered his tender white feet across the gravel to the crossbars of the TV antenna where his best suit-coat clanged back and forth on its hanger in the wind. So that his wife could get a better view of the sky, Mr. Davis leaned out over the edge of the roof and, with a pair of hedge clippers borrowed from Mr. Cochrane, began to trim the overhanging tree branches. Behind him, Mr. Cochrane -- who sold automobile mufflers for a living and who covered the bald spot on the top of his head with a dab of Brindle Brothers shoe polish -- held on with both hands to Mr. Davis' belt to keep him from falling. The average year-round temperature in Florida is 70° Fahrenheit. Even as we speak another hundred head of cattle are being born.

Jack slid down from his father's arms and onto the crate of Campbell's Cream of Mushroom Soup the Landfair girls were unpacking. Janet Landfair, the younger of the two, the pretty one, brushed the sleep from his eyes and told him to go play but to keep away from the edge. She'd been taking a bath. Her hair was still damp, her skin smooth as a wet pebble. She smelled like a bowl of fresh strawberries, and as she turned back to the check-list at her feet, she pressed a can of Chicken Vegetable into his arms and brushed the top of his head with a kiss. Jack closed his eyes and slowly lifted his head, like in the movies, like when they touch, with a sword, the top of the head of King Arthur. She was gone by the time he opened his eyes. He could just make out the sound of her voice, chirping away with some girls back the other side of the chimney. Arthur comes from the Celtic word *artos*, meaning "bear." The peanut is a vegetable.

The peanut is a vegetable. Jack knelt down to tie his sneakers, then climbed up onto a big Philco box TV that somebody had managed to wrestle up onto one of the far corners of the roof. How strange to see all the different families in their loose individual orbits around the other families, the Dad trotting out to the edge and then back again across the gravel to the family pile – TV tray, thermos jug, bed-sheet, hula-hoop, screwdriver, hair-dryer, bug-spray, pretzels – and how strange it all up in the sky like that with no drawer and no closets to keep the wind from mixing it together: old Mr. Porter rummaging through a crateful of oranges for a matching blue sock, somebody's pink flamingo salt shaker mixed in with somebody else's number four lug nuts, a bowling shoe with a big red "9" on the heel and a swizzle-stick wedged into the laces, a Koo-Ade pitcher filled with goldfish, a hatbox full of dog biscuits, three red cabbages in a skin-diver's mask and everybody looking down and over the edge to the little box houses that they had just broken out of.

It was the end of the world. Mrs. Goodman (belt buckle long since disappeared into the curve of her gut) leaned out over her potato salad to glimpse – above the smolder of moss that muddied the oak -- that sliver-of-a-tangerine moon. Out among the picnic baskets and the hardware tools and the cans of buttered Mexicali corn, Barbara Sego stopped to straighten the curlers in her hair and to wipe her hands on the back of her tight white shorts. She looked back to see that Mr. Goodman was watching, then called out to ask him could he, would he, just for a tiny second, push this box of roofing nails out of the way for her? The men on either side of Mr. G swayed and swayed as she spoke, sang out in soft high voices *oh would you, could you, would you?* as Mr. G, wrench in hand, scrambled out from under his barbecue grill and stumbled to his feet. The stirrup is the smallest bone in the body. Barbeque was first invented in 1526.

Easy now. Jack fingered, hooked with his little finger the antenna of the Philco to keep his balance. As the wind climbed up and over the horizon to the west, the stars seemed to rise and to fall with it, as if they were riding a tide, as if the sky itself were about to buckle. To the east? Sunrise. Sky the color of rose, and all of the families – fidgeting and bickering and chattering – practically bursting up to meet it. Or so it seemed to Jack from his perch on the edge of the darkness. The people they looked fresh and they looked tattered at the very same time, like a batch of presents torn open on a Christmas morning or a crowd spilling down the exit ramp of the Tilt-'O-Whirl, like the morning last fall when the whole neighborhood suddenly, in the middle of breakfast, jumped up and ran out into the street – barefoot or with one sock on, spoon in the mouth, face half-full of shaving cream or no make-up or soggy hair or cold cigarette stuck to the face and the pants half-zipped in a one-legged run – everybody pulled out to the street by the high wailing screech of Miss Overman on her knees with her arms around the back tire of a Milk Truck from The Gustafson Farms Dairy, Mama and Papa Gus smiling down at her from a side panel mural and smiling out again across the neighborhood from the opposite side of the truck, the crowd closing in, the cries rising up, the driver in his milk-colored overalls six feet back both arms gesturing and waving *get away get away* as if creating some kind of wind that could blow Miss Overman back away from his truck and from the obliterated body of her pet cat Pluto. How strange it was to see everyone flushed out into the open like that, all of their gear in a tangle at their feet, all of their sociable clothes abandoned. The can of soup slipped out of Jack's hand and landed in the gutter with a clang. The closest planet to the sun is Mercury.

    Everybody was busy with something. The Cochrane's Irish Setter Spike had one of Janet's curlers in his mouth and as he ran back and forth along the edge of the roof with his nose in the air, sniffing, Michael Cochrane chased after him with a ball of kite string in one hand and a garden rake in the other. Mrs. Harrison with her stiff gray hair was trying to set up a card table on the windward side of the chimney, but as soon as she got the one leg anchored, the other gave way. Jack was trying to figure out where that Porter baby had gotten hold of a chocolate chip cookie. The Bowhead whale filters thousands of gallons of seawater through the sieve of the mouth for every pound of plankton it obtains.

The end. The end of the world. Jack buttoned the collar of his Roy Rogers pajamas and carefully made his way along the roof's edge. The gravel crackled underfoot, the branches of the pines raked back and forth against the cinder-block houses, the smell of orange blossom and burnt rubber flashed by as the wind gusted, and paused, and gusted again. Jack remembered his father telling him how the bulldozers had to be careful when they first invented the street, how they'd try not to smash into these pines because of the name of the street – Pine Street. And the palmettos, the palmettos in Palmetto Court. The name like a picture. Like the name of the road round the corner there, Orange Grove Road? No. No. They built it out of a orange grove, but when the time came to name it they discovered a mistake, that this was not the picture they'd wanted, they'd need a new picture, that in their rush to build the road they'd plowed under all the oranges. So they had to name it "Hernando," Hernando Drive so as not to put a dent in the overall view, Hernando in honor of the Spanish conquistador Hernando De Soto who swung by Florida in 1539 after sailing 5,000 miles across the Atlantic Ocean. "Gentleman Jim" Corbett is the name of a famous American Heavyweight Boxing Champion from the 1890s. Many breeds of dog are descended from a single Boston Terrier.

There was a rumbling in the distance. The sky grew lighter. Jack's father handed him a pair of fingernail clippers and told him to clip his nails so that he would not look like he'd just crawled in out the woods. The steering wheel of a 1964 Chevy Impala appeared at the top of the ladder, followed by a hand around the steering column like the hand was just along for the ride. It was T-Bird Wilson whose mother had died and left him the house on the corner last year while he was away in the army. He jogged quickly to the far end of the roof where he drove the steering column into a laundry exhaust pipe and then climbed up onto the wheel like it was a stool in a bar. As the birds blew by in the wind he whirled and raised his hands to his face and pretended to shoot at them.

Everybody was busy with something. Fat Mr. Deverall rose up over the sharp edge of the roof, the ladder sagging gently under this weight as he climbed, the rungs creaking in a rhythm with the grunt of his voice, as if the ladder was a musical instrument and he was the tune it was playing. Somebody had swept away enough of the gravel to spread out a red checkered picnic blanket where Mrs. Cochrane (angry at her husband for having awakened her in the first place) lay snoring with an embroidered tea-cloth across her face. Mr. Cochrane's job was to wake his wife when the time came so that she would not miss anything. Tea-cloths were first embroidered by the British in the 1700s. Over seven thousand separate sugar cane stalks go into the production of a single drop of chocolate.

The men dropped a bungee cord into the mist. Tried to hook the garden hose – there, upside the house there, still fat with the force of the water, the sprinkler a-spin – but wait. Mrs. Harrison called out to say *wait, but wait*, that whoever wanted to wash up, that she had a canteen and here, a hubcap, T-Bird's hubcap for a sink. Not so good as a cooler, a Styrofoam cooler but no, too late, it was too late for that. When the Porter's baby began to cry they'd made a cradle of it, laid him in the bottom with a few dishtowels and Mr. Dentiston's sweat-shirt as a mattress. It was the end of the world.

Jack listened to the clanging of the tetherball pole in the backyard and wished that he'd gone back to get the globe of the world that was hanging from the ceiling of his bedroom. The globe was made out of an old tetherball the countries of which Jack had painted in by hand – the democracies in green, the communists in red, the oceans of the world in indigo blue. Cornelius J. Crowley Jr. of New Haven, Connecticut invented the molded-rubber-with-lacing tetherball in 1956. Admiral

Perry was a great man. Running out from the top of the pole and into the smashed-up center of an old orange tree was Jack's mother's clothesline with the laundry flapping in the gray light and the branches of the pines roaring and roaring around it. The clothes in a ripsaw -- Jack's mother had forgotten to grab them -- but still, it was nice to look down, and to think of them as flags, personal individual flags, a line of banners in the wind like the signal flags on the bow of a ship.

Most of the people on the roof were still in their pajamas. Jack's father had on the pinstripe pajamas that Jack had gotten him in honor of Joe DiMaggio number 9 of the New York Yankees, son of a crab fisherman and the only player in the history of the game to hit safely in 56 consecutive games. Jack's father's father immigrated from Croatia in the days of the Kaiser. He was a cook on one of Teddy Roosevelt's expeditions to Africa.

Old Mr. Cottles wandered over to Jack with one slipper off and a red toothbrush at the end of his shaking fingers. He had gotten hold of his wife's toothbrush by accident and now he didn't want to use it for fear of the germs. It had taken him a long time to climb up to the top of the ladder and now there were these blue streaks of toothpaste smeared up and down the front of his terry-cloth bathrobe. Jack took him around to each one of the families in turn to ask for a new toothbrush.

A low fog came rolling in across the trim lawns and into the mailboxes and around and over the chain link fences between the separate homes. Up top of the last remaining ladder sat the paperboy with his legs disappearing over the edge of the roof like it was a raft in the middle of great gray ocean. At the foot of the drive a fire hydrant. Slung over the snout a haversack. A dozen papers, rolled and rubber-banded into little log shapes, spilled out the sack and onto the lawn, the drive, and onto the spokes of the Schwinn Glider the paperboy had – like a rodeo rider – abandoned on the fly. His flashlight flicked on and off as he slapped it with the palm of his hand. The highest waterfall in the world is Angel Falls in Venezuela. Africa is the third largest continent.

Next to the paperboy was a policeman. He'd come up with his equipment, but one good look at the distant tree line – bristled up and vibrating in the wind like the fur on the back of a bear – and he tossed the gun and the walkie-talkie overboard. The azalea bush crackled with invisible voices. Jack elbowed his way to the edge. Miss Overman's brittle hairdo brushed his arm as he leaned over to listen. Azalea. It was an azalea blossom Miss Overman laid, launched, lofted into Pluto's waterbowl the day the truck, all a-jangle with milk, struck him. On the hinge of his left arm the milkman had had a tattoo of a hinge that he'd gotten in Japan just after the war. Jack wondered what the milkman was doing now. McArthur was a great general.

McArthur was a great general. Before he threw the gun away, the policeman took out the bullets and passed them around to the kids as souvenirs. The handcuffs he clamped onto the ladder and the rain gutter so that nobody would lose their balance and get pitched out into the flowerbed below.

The clouds swept in so smoothly as they brushed the tops of the trees, it seemed the sky itself was standing still and it was the gray gravel roof that was doing the gliding. Somebody had brought up a thermos of coffee and it was making the rounds. Mr. Straley had a backpack with a side pocket full of sugar and Sweet'N Low in little packets. To stir with, Renee Coats broke out some tiny plastic spoons and knives from her Barbie Doll set.

Bobby Straley leaned against the chimney in his red pajamas and used a baseball glove to brush the gravel out from between his toes. He always carried his glove with him everywhere because he was afraid that somebody would steal it.

Sally Goodman had her crayons and a couple sheets of manila paper spread out across the Harrison's wobbly card table. She was making a drawing of the streaks of red and yellow breaking out across the sky from left to right.

Jack's father stood in a circle with the other fathers and chewed on a blue plastic toothpick and scratched his earlobe and looked down and then up and then down again as he listened to the other fathers talk. The fathers had decided that it was time to break out the ponchos in case it rained, but Jack's father argued that after all it was fairly warm out and what, were they made out of sugar or something and what, was a couple drops of water going to kill them? Why couldn't they just let it rain? The men thought that this was a good idea, so they tossed the ponchos over the edge.

Bonnie Flightstone had a Instamatic but she didn't have any flashcubes left. She was going around to all of the families asking them if they had any extras. The Porter baby had one in his mouth but by the time they pried it loose the plastic plug-in part was all twisted up and would no longer fit into the slot of Bonnie's camera. Griffin Porter told her that it wasn't much use anyway because the most you could hope to capture with a flash would be, what, eight, eight and a half feet. What the hell you gonna get at eight and a half feet?

Jack spread his father's jacket out on the gravel and got down on his belly to see through the window of the Dentiston's living room two doors down. The lights were off but the TV was on, a small cube of light in the corner. Mr. D knelt alongside as Jack adjusted the binoculars they'd borrowed from the Landfairs. In the two circles of the binoculars he could see that there was some kind of morning wake up show going on inside of Mr. D's TV. A man was standing in front of a picture of a tree. He was holding up a fishing pole and casting it out into an imaginary stream. Mr. D had clicked onto the show but then turned off the sound so that he could read by the dim light without waking Mrs. D, who was sleeping in the living room because she was afraid of the mouse in the bedroom, Mr. D's pet mouse in the blue plastic cage they'd brought up onto the roof with them when they found out it was going to be the end of the world.

Everybody was helping themselves to a big wooden salad bowl filled with peanuts that Jack's mother had placed on top of the chimney. Since this was Florida where the average year-round temperature is 70° F, the chimney was a fake chimney, aluminum with red paint so that from the street it would look like a giant brick sticking up out of the roof. The aluminum was molded by Vernon Dewald, a friend of Jack's father who came to Florida from West Virginia in 1952 and who set up his aluminum shop alongside the furniture warehouse on Silver Star Road. The largest silver mine in the world is in Queensland, Australia. The only way to get a chigger-bug out from under your skin is to rub alcohol on it. Because of the trouble that Jack's mom had gone to, most everybody, the grown-ups especially, tried – as they shucked the peanuts – to toss the shells into the wicker basket she'd anchored to the chimney with a swatch of duct tape.

Mr. Terry sat in his bathrobe on the edge of a folding lawn chair with a flashlight and the Orlando Morning Sentinel (*'Tis A Privilege To Live In Central Florida*) spread out across his knees. The official motto of the city of Orlando is "The City Beautiful." The amoeba is likely to turn up anywhere at any time in any random drop of water. Some of the neighborhood kids gathered around Mr. Terry to watch him finish up the crossword puzzle on page seven next to the box scores of the Orlando Twins, Triple-A farm team of the famous Minnesota Twins organization who do their playing at Tinker Field – named after Tinker of Tinkers-to-Evers-to-Chance – and who move their whole operation down here once a year for spring training.

77

Joe Lena and his wife Tammy stood near the top of the ladder arguing about whether or not Joe had forgotten to turn off the stove when they left. Joe had a cup of coffee in his hand and Tammy was pointing at it and telling Joe that there must have been somewhere that he had gotten that from and that it was hot wasn't it and if he would take the trouble to look around him did he happen to see anybody up here roasting marshmallows around a roaring fire? Joe is nodding his head and sipping coffee and looking out at the streaks of red climbing up out of the clouds in the east. Joe is telling Tammy that she is being a perfect example of the word that she is always accusing him of calling her, but Tammy is insisting to Joe that if they don't want to see their little nest-egg reduced to a pile of cinders then they had better be paying some attention. Joe cups his hands over the coffee to keep it warm and presses his lips between his fingers for another sip as he watches the streak of red against the gray sky grow.

Jack is nudging Johnny Goodman with the heel of his cowboy boot and trying to loosen the package of firecrackers from Johnny's back pocket, Mr. Terry is scratching the word "Antipodal" into the margin of his newspaper, Tammy Lena is tucking her lime green polyester blouse into the waistband of her panty hose, Vernon Dewald is leaning out over the round eyes of the Porter baby and making a clucking sound with his tongue between his teeth, Bob Dentiston is trying to drape his windbreaker across the blue cage of his pet mouse Oscar, the Southwestern Desert Kangaroo Rat living as it does on the moisture in its solid food is the only mammal capable of living completely without drinking water for many years on end, Mrs. Dentiston stands beside her husband with a bobby pin in her mouth, the state song of Florida is "The Swanee River," Mrs. Goodman has Jay by the collar and is wiping the streak of Hershey's Chocolate Syrup from his cheek with a wet rag, Mr. Goodman is telling Mr. Cochrane the story about the Bootlegger and the Librarian and the Landfair girls are squatting above the cans of Cream of Asparagus pretending not to listen, Mrs. Straley is telling Bobby if he doesn't stop throwing gravel at the chimney she's going to take his "Newk" Newcombe autograph model and pitch it over the edge, Donald Newcombe is the first black major league pitcher of the modern era to win more than 20 games in a season, the women are folding baby clothes and debating how long it will take for Bob Dentiston to make another pass at that Sego woman and the men are standing at the edge of the roof smoking and pointing to the huge red rent across the face of the eastern sky the clouds disappearing into it the first Republican governor of Florida Harrison Reed in 1868 and Jack trying to peel open the packet of Black Cat firecrackers before Johnny Goodman has a chance to catch him at it even as you read it coming to the world as all things must or try as you might and nothing you it coming to can or would say the end.

Winner - Vincent Brothers Review 2020 Short Story Contest
Appeared in Vincent Brothers Review Issue #24 Spring 2021

THE GREYHOUND

by Alan Sincic

We all of us like to believe, now and again, when the body blooms with the vigor of the earth, that the whole of who we are is an *ex nihilo* creation, that we sprout up like mushrooms after rain, fresh from out the mind of the Almighty. But then you stub the toe or crack the knuckle or rub the palm of the hand up over the brass marker atop a grave and wham, there you go again, back into the skin you got from all the kin that come before, the flesh and the blood at the start of it all.

I know. I know. Nothing special here. Everybody got a genesis. But if you think of that self of yours a precious thing (and don't lie to me now, you do), then it stands to reason even me, made from the same stuff as you, got just as good a cause to call myself, if not precious, then at the very least, a – what would be the word? – remarkable event. A moment worthy of a marker.

So mark. Mark this. You got a he. You got a she. She grows up in a two-story wood frame house perched on a hill overlooking the Cleveland Zoo. A city street of clap-board houses, booming up close enough to string a clothesline from roof to roof but, by some accident of geography, bounded on three sides (just this one street, this cul de sac) by open space. The valley – ravine, really – sweeps around in a horseshoe shape, the railroad on the one flank, the rear of the zoo on the other. Now and again hobos'll trudge uphill from the train tracks to knock on the back door. For a few pennies or a meal, they chop the wood or haul the ice or patch the broken trellis. On winter nights the family gathers in the kitchen beside the stove – the only warmth – to read aloud from Emerson or the Post or the tales of Arthur Conan Doyle. Come the summer she sits at the upstairs bedroom window. Out over the far dark she gazes. The sliver moon. The molten Cuyahoga where it slugs round the base of a hill. On the city side, off a half-mile maybe, the broken molar of the brick tower and the factory and the tenement. On the near side -- across a gap of empty black, heavy with myrtle -- the seals bray, the monkeys yowl, the lions roar.

    He grows up in a Croat ghetto on the south side of Detroit, shuffles from home to home after the death of his dad in the great flu epidemic of the Twenties. He and his brother sleep on a pallet on the floor of a basement – this the tale he tells me when I ask about the life he lived: the rats that scurry across the covers as they sleep, the toys they cobble outta scraps of tin, the bone soup, the bread the flavor of brick. He hoboes cross-country, joins the CC's to fight floods and forest fires, then the forest service, then the army at the outbreak of war, then the injury, the years in the hospital, till finally... college on the GI Bill.

    1952. He's near to the end of college when his mother dies. He buys a bus ticket from Gainesville to Detroit for the funeral. She's near to the end of vacation with friends in Miami, the money for the plane she gives way to a friend in need, so she's gotta hurry now, gotta trek back to her teaching job in Cleveland. The story begins (so say the makers of me) in Miami, where she boards the *SunMaid*. It seems there are a pair of busses, actually -- the *SunMaid* and the *SunKing* – that travel north from Florida together -- a caravan. One follows the other and they stop, at the same time, at the same depots and filling stations and roadside diners all the way up the spine of the Appalachians and into the Midwest. She almost misses the bus – has to run the last block to the station. It's crowded. She's lucky to get a seat. That same evening he boards the *SunKing* in Gainesville, and the two Greyhounds roll out onto the dark highway together for the long journey to Columbus. There the busses will part company, go their separate ways, spill their riders out where the random wander.

    In those days there is no interstate, so the roads have to climb up and down the hills, wind themselves round the mountains, glide down into the small towns where the houses crowd in right up to the curbside and you can look out and see the people on their porch swings in the evening, the kids pitching pennies and chasing fireflies or perched on the porch railing, squabbling about who gets the funnies or who stole the last cookie. You can crack a window, sliver the wind, smell the tobacco leaf crackle in the sun, the char of a blown gasket out the pit of a passing garage, the crush of cedar mulch and rhododendron, the button-brush and cypress and creosote as the bus splinters up over the corduroy bridge at the edge of town.

Such a long trip. Do the same pair of drivers handle the whole route? How can they possibly drive for thirty-six hours? Do they swap out every ten hours, Pony Express style? The Florida driver surrenders to the Georgia driver, Georgia driver to the mountain driver, mountain driver to the... who knows? You surrender to the bus. That's the way it's done. You sleep or read or smoke or talk while it carries you on to wherever it promised it would go, like children surrender when they doze off in the car and then wake, in the morning, in their own bed.

So on they travel on their separate busses. Somewhere outside Macon, Georgia, and late – midnight maybe – the busses pull in for gas and the passengers trickle off. A chance to shake out the kinks, shoulder out into the open, grab a smoke or a cup of coffee. On her way in through the diner door – picture one of those heavy glass and chrome and steel things – she pops open her purse to fish for a nickel. In those days you can get a pack of Lifesavers or a Coke or a clutch of fries for a nickel. And then it happens. As she retrieves the nickel, a something flutters out the purse without her seeing.

So go the laws of physics. Paper floats. Doors open and close. All my life I've pictured it: the cushion of air and the puff as the door shuts, the weight of the brass and of the air itself as you suction it open, the swirl of the heat of the people on the inside and the cool of the stars in the dark on the outside, then the place where the cool and the warm -- just on the threshold, the coming and the going -- collide. I lean closer. I close my eyes. I try to picture the thing that can't be pictured: the invisible hand that plucks a five dollar bill from out a purse half-opened and then, at precisely the right moment, drops it to the curb.

A fiver. For five bucks in 1952 you can buy 165 postage stamps, or sixteen gallons of gas, or five Porterhouse steaks. A dog. A leather jacket. A bleacher-seat ticket to the World Series. Or you can spend it out over a whole day if you want -- a shoeshine, a haircut, a monogrammed hankie, a fifty-pound pumpkin, a box of Tide, five pounds of sugar and an all-you-can-eat fried chicken dinner served family style with tomato juice, shrimp cocktail, relish dish, salad bowl, hot biscuit, mashed potatoes, cream gravy, string beans, your choice pie or ice cream + (non-alcoholic) drink.

Or out over a whole lifetime – twenty-seven shares ATT&T @ 78 cents/share plus compound interest over 60 years. Or nothing. You tread it underfoot. A candy wrapper. A collar stay. A broken leaf. You could. He could. But he doesn't.

He stops. Picks it up. Taps her on the shoulder. She thanks him, they chat, he flirts, and – all aboard – off they go, each to a bus of their own.

Somewhere further up the road, hours later, the busses pull in for breakfast. One of those roadside diners with the ribbon of counter and the Budweiser clock and the silver-brim, button-mushroom stools, like the knobby bumpers a pinball rides on its way down the slopes. North Carolina. The place empty. She's got a headache. Not a morning person. Twenty-plus hours on this bus, this box made of steel, and stuffed with strangers, and sealed shut. She deliberately seeks out the farthest stool from the door, swivels round to face the wall, props her elbow up on the counter, and cradles her cheek in the palm of her hand.

In he comes and – just as deliberately – passes all the empty stools to plant himself beside her. The ketchup and the mustard in the glass jars, silos of salt and pepper and sugar, the porcelain creamer and the matchbook caddy and the shot glass jammed with toothpicks, all clacked up into a tableau, every six feet an ensemble – the napkin a cloud, the ashtray a manger, the stub of the Lucky Strike a baby Jesus there smoldering in the moonlight.

Who knows how – through what alchemy – vinegar turns to wine, but by the end of breakfast they move beyond a hello. Not friendship – you don't measure that in minutes – but surely something. He tries to cajole, to beg, to bribe the bus driver into letting him swap busses so that he can ride with her. It is not to be. They must live by the laws the Order of The Greyhound decrees: ten-minute rest stops, meals on the fly, bits and scraps of conversation.

Before they reach Columbus, he manages to extract from her a promise. In Columbus he has to transfer to a bus heading north to Detroit. She has a short layover before her connecting bus to Cleveland. If she would take a later bus, then they could spend an hour or two together in Columbus – take a walk, talk, have some dinner – before heading their separate ways.

So the *SunMaid* arrives in Columbus. She disembarks and waits at the station for the *SunKing* to arrive. And waits. And waits. She knows his name, but they've yet to exchange phone numbers and addresses. She barely even knows the guy. And here now at the depot – here's the bus to Cleveland. She's got the ticket. If she boards it now, in two hours it'll be over. Instead of camping for hours on a bench for a guy who might not even show, she'll be home. The hot bath, the clean sheets, the soft bed. And it's not like she owes him. What they'd agreed to was a meal. But that trick with the length of twine. That was funny. That was sweet. How you loop it round your fingers, just so, pull it taut, thread to thread, to snap it. Snaps in half! How keen to show her – like a boy – but, at the same time, what would be the word? Courtly. As if serving up, not a trick of the twist of a finger, but a treasure.

Is it the trick that tilts her back a step to where he's waiting, that nudges him on a step, into the light, into her favor? A glint of wind in the surge of a stream to you, gentle reader, comfy reader, who sit snug in the vessel of flesh you got from God knows where, but to me a momentous occasion.

> ❝ He woke. It was nothing, he figured. Wind is what? Wind is air. And air is what? Air is – put your hand out. Give it a shake. Nothing. Air is nothing.

Courtly. That's the word. And his mother has died. And a promise is a promise. So she gambles. She waits.

When the *SunKing* finally pulls into Columbus – a full hour late – he climbs off with a sack of potatoes in hand. There'd been an accident. A truck overturned. Potatoes everywhere. While the cops and the tow-trucks sort the mess, he roams out onto the roadway. Gathers up the swag. The hunter home from the hill.

So how do we mark it? The moment? Look. Come look. Not but a half century later. We got me and my brother. My sisters. The seed of the he and the she. And we all of us got kids of our own, and some of these grown, and with babies on the way, and we all of us racing on to rendezvous we never planned, and here's the way we mark the grave –

an embossment in brass of a greyhound.

    The logo of the Greyhound's a dog in a sprint, right? Slim as a drift of air. Even in brass, here beneath the palm of the hand, it's got the feel of something – what would be the word? – fleet. Fleeting. On the fly.

    Take it for what it's worth, but remarkable is what we say.

Winner - 2023 Plentitudes Prize in Nonfiction
Appeared online in The Plentitudes Special Awards Issue Spring 2023

IF YOU'RE COLD, THEY'RE COLD

BY AARON MORRISON

Mommy. It's cold.

The child's voice echoes from behind the thick, wooden door, through the foyer and into the living room, permeating the sound of the crackling fire, the screaming wind encircling the house, and the rattling of the snow caked windows.

Elizabeth rises from her armchair.

"Where are you going?" Henry asks.

"It's our boy," Elizabeth answers, looking at Henry with confused and sunken eyes.

"Elizabeth." Henry says her name in tender firmness. "Our son is gone. Whatever is out there, it's not our Thomas."

Mommy. It's cold.

"Don't you recognize our son's voice? How can we leave him out there?" Elizabeth pleads.

"We can. And we will. Because it's not him."

"You are a cruel, cruel man."

"Why? Because I have accepted the loss of our son?"

"You don't understand a mother's grief."

"Perhaps not. But do you think that the loss of him has not broken me? Or that I don't long to have our son back?"

"I've prayed every night that God would return him to us." Elizabeth's shoulders sink.

"If whatever's out there is a response to prayer, it wasn't God who answered."

"You're right." Elizabeth nods, walks to the whiskey decanter, pours a drink, and hands it to Henry.

"Thank you." Henry drinks, not tasting what Elizabeth added, and is soon unconscious.

Frigid wind passes through her useless shawl as Elizabeth opens the door.

She looks down at the small, hideous form grinning up at her with sharp, glistening, translucent teeth.

Mommy. It's cold.

THE SMILE CONTEST

BY ALAN SINCIC

The children gathered along the back wall of Miss Connor's class in a line that would have been—were it not for the cracks in the blue linoleum floor—perfectly straight. One crack in particular stirred in Farrel a desire.

It looked like a volcanic ridge from out the bed of an ocean. Into the crevasse where the tile pooched upward he thrust the tip of a sneaker. Wriggled the foot. Crowbarred at the broken flooring. The white rubber cap of the shoe—already loosened to a hinge from a season of play—peeled off completely. Scalped. He kicked at the shred of white. Strike one. Kicked again. It pogo-ed off down the aisle between the tiny desks.

"Farrel?" Miss Connor always sang, not the name of the child, but the syllables that made the name, as if the name were the opening bar to a melody she'd been trying, for the life of her, to remember. "Are you one of my Old Faithfuls?"

"Yes, ma'am."

"You are?"

"Yes, ma'am."

"Then who was that Silly Willy I just saw from out the corner of my eye?"

"I don't know, ma'am. It weren't me."

"Glad to hear it. Then would you be so kind as to fetch that little scrap of something or other I just saw from out the other corner of my eye?"

"Yes, ma'am."

And so he did.

"That was so gallant of you," said Miss Connor as she fingered the scrap of rubber. She smiled. "It would be so nice if you could do me one more thing."

Farrel nodded. Gallant. He didn't know what it meant exactly—

something about brave—but it burned in a gentle way. If you could slip on a skin made out of cinnamon, that's what it would feel like. A cinnamon skin.

"If you could be the line-watcher, that would be so nice." Miss Connor pointed to the back of the line. The children snickered. "What we want," she said to the class in a melodious drawl, "is a line with no wrinkles."

A special line to match the special day. The apple of the earth all ruddy with the dawn. The birds piping and the crisp of the cloud and the chill breath of a moon over yonder in the dark. Today the day of the Smile Contest. The children felt the stir of something new from the moment the truck pulled into the lot beside the lunchroom. Like a mail-truck painted white, the big kind, you know, or like a Ice Cream wagon with the panel flanks and the bay in the back big enough to juggle puppies in.

The King of Ice Cream. That's the way Farrel pictured himself. Gliding, smooth as a bar of soap, between the green hills of Ohio and into the little towns like Smallville in the days of Superboy or whatever they called that neighborhood Dick and Jane and Sally and Spot in the reader all rambled around in. Run, Spot, Run! He would live in the truck, and in the white dungarees with the broad pockets and the white jacket and shirt and the silver change-maker strapped to the belly like a belt of ammo, and the children would all come running when he'd roll down the lane with a ring of the bell and a wave of the hand but he wouldn't stop, no, he'd stand at the back counter, high above the back bumper, in the center of the sign with the pictures of Cherry Pops and Push-Ups and Heath Bars and Dreamsicles he'd toss, one after another, out the back and into the arms of the children on their bikes and their skateboards and their skinny scabby legs. His robot would drive the truck for him. Major Domo. That would be the name he'd give it, the robot name. Every night, camped on the edge of town or in a secret cave or on the top of a mountain, he would tinker with The Major to add even more features. A squirt gun of a thumb. Jet pack. Laser Vision.

* * * * * *

With the lightest of touch—a shoulder, a sleeve, a tap on the brow—Miss Conner uncoupled the line of children from the lip of the window that ran the length of the room. To the water-fountain, the pencil sharpener, the bathroom—the sign of the red STOP and, on the flip side, the green GO—she herded them.

Back to the window she turned. Drew the hankie from her apron pocket. Made a show of it, like the dusting of the window was a daily event, like the man in the truck, should he glance in her direction, would see it as a natural thing, a consequence of the breath, a woman of a mind to—at the break of the day and the brim of the glass—give it a shine.

The man clicked the handle of the sliding door on the passenger side and, as it shouldered open, stepped out onto the running board. He looked back at the emblem on the side panel, reached under the seat for a rag, then down he hopped. Set to work.

The emblem was a tooth the size of a couch, a cartoon molar with cartoony blue eyes and a smiley mouth and bean-sprouty little arms and legs like pins in a cushion, like a toothpick in a aperitif. The man wiped the dust off the emblem with his rag, then wiped the dust off his shoes, then, with the back of his hand, wiped the sweat from his brow. He was a young man. He moved with that extra bit of oomph the young give to all of them extra moves they make. He donned the white blazer—the lab jacket off the rack in the back of the truck—with an extra flourish. Snapped the collar. Snapped the cuffs. He was a handsome fella, and he took pride in this thing he'd accomplished, this handsomeness. And the clipboard he carried, snug up under the arm? A list of the classes he planned to favor with a visit. He gave the box—the big box full of toothbrushes and flyers and fingerling tubes of toothpaste—an extra jounce on his way up the steps of the school.

Handsome is as handsome does, right? Miss Connor clapped her hands to hurry the children along. She was (in her own words) a handsome woman. Not pretty. Not (God no) sexy. Nicely framed. That would be the word. The handsome was not about her but about the order she gathered around her. That was the important thing. On her way out the house she'd always touch the frame of the door beneath the glint of the paint. Rub the grain of the wood, special order from the sawmill and why not, if that was her impulse, to own a scrap of something raw, the roughcut timber with the half-circle scored, the same shape, score upon score, up the doorpost and over the lintel in the house with the wooden floors and the Shaker chairs and the doormat fashioned, or so the vendor said, from a bolt of virgin wool. Handsome, see? Of the hands. The broken ripple where the blade meets the pine. She'd feel it there under her fingers when she'd cradle the frame, just so, when she'd loose the cat from out the house and over the stoop and into the blue of the day.

The blue of the day. The white of the truck. The sun that breaks over the pines to strike the—like in the ads for Duz with the extra oounch of whitening—vehicle. White like the flesh of a coconut, the flank of a glacier, the ingot of fire from out the heart of the moon.

"Farrel?" Miss Connor said it in the form of a question, but it was bigger than where is your pencil or what's in your pocket or even what are

> **The wooden flag from off a mailbox. The collar from off a dog. The sock you fill with sand to sling—a sock-rocket—up into the blue. Private things. Snatch of underwear from off a neighbor's line.**

you doing? It was an open window, the question. Fling open the shutters to summon the wind. "Bring me that, please."

The that was a note. He'd snatched it from the Bergdahl girl and held it now, two-handed, behind his back. For the past minute Miss Connor (from out the corner of her eye) had followed the dance of the boy and the girl, the thrust and the parry. Prim little thing, Martha Nell, with the saddle shoes and the socks that pinched her in the plummy red of the flesh. She pecked at the note. Like a bobbin on a spindle, Farrel spun left, then right, then left again. Just out of reach he held it.

"Farrel!"

Farrel marched himself up the aisle and into the dock. Farrel-land the children called it, the patch of the flooring at the far corner of her desk where he stood to attention day after day, two, three times a day to once again—as Miss Connor called it—explain himself.

A haven. A land of milk and honey. He'd rest his chin on the wooden edge of the desk while he waited for her to rule, smell the varnish and the Pinesol and the coffee, rock his head from side to side, sticky up onto his cheeks the pencil shavings and the diblets of rubber eraser as he watched and as he waited. It was all of it familiar, homey even, the spot on the floor. His spot. Here. Where the bad children stand to await the day of judgement, where the soles of their feet sand the tile down to a tar the width of a cookie.

Over the course of the year Miss Connor had commandeered from him the hamster bone, the broken crayon, the penknife, the Rocket Racer, sparrow feather, bottle cap, gyroscope, platoon of plastic army men with the magnifying glass to weld them into a burl of prickly green.

"That's the price you pay," she'd told him, the sermon she'd offered up with every collar, "when you take from others." She would always pause here, for emphasis, after the manner of Winston Churchill. "When you trespass a territory not your own, there's a price you pay." She would elevate the sinful object, hold it there for him to see, to value, to weigh in the balance beside the what? Devilment is what. Chimpery. Animal spirits. The invisible whim and the twitch of the nerve and the hum of the blood.

On the shelf behind her, out of reach but in sight, there, beside the antique barometer and the biscuit tin all clanky with crayons? A season of loot. On the first day of school he'd smuggled a box of candy cigarettes into the library. Pall Mall (Whenever The Finest Is Desired), with the logo the crest of the king with the armor, and the red pepper of the lions, and the burst of the yellow star with the Toy Surprise Inside! "This little item." She gave it a shiver, like you shake a tin of cocoa to tally the mass. "You want it back, right?"

"Yes, ma'am."

"Good. Then here's the deal, okay? You get it back the day the shenanigans end."

So much for noble intent. Day by day the collection grew. The wooden flag from off a mailbox. The collar from off a dog. The sock you fill with sand to sling—a sock-rocket—up into the blue. Private things. Snatch of underwear from off a neighbor's line. Birthday card with a blot for a name. The thing he found in the bottom drawer of her desk that day before school, him looking for nothing he could think of in particular apart

from it belonging to her is all. Finders Keepers, right? She'd stepped out to shoo the squirrels away from the hummingbird feeder. Like it was the fault of the squirrel for being the squirrel and not the feeder for being the feeder, right out in the open like that, the red of the raspberry jam.
Tampax the letters in a mimeo blue up the seam of the white paper wrapper. A kind of a cigar is what he figured it was, that or a packet of que-tips. Whatever. It crackled when he pressed it, with the pad of his thumb, into the lunchbox, into the crevasse where the apple and the PBJ and the Have Gun Will Travel thermos nestled. Clicked the lid shut. He took it why? He couldn't say. Half of what he did he did from out a hankering to fill the empty hand. That's the whole point of a touch, right? To touch.

So no wonder then, when he showed up the next day, how smitten she was by his boldery.

"How becoming you look," she said as the children arrived in their Halloween gear, the class for the party, Farrel in the cardboard armor he'd elbowed into shape from out a box of Idaho potatoes.

"Space armor," he said. "A robot is what I am."

From an old bucket of Kentucky Fried Chicken he'd fashioned a helmet. Slits for the eyes. Gawp of a mouth like a Jack O' Lantern. The tin from a chicken pot pie torqued up at a angle and glued to the top. Radar! The Tampax he'd positioned between the eyes and stapled into place. She reddened when she saw it but said nothing.

Had she known where he'd gotten it, she would have what? Done what? Given him what in return? A gold star? A kiss? A crack on the noggin to go with the licks he got from that mother of his?
What she did was this, Miss Connor, what she figured was this: he'd fumbled up onto this little piece of feminine magic from out of a dresser at home, that's what he'd done, or back of the bath towels, or up top the linens. Or no. No. That would be too easy. She pictured him a shoplifter on the run, boss of the supermarket bulling up the aisle behind him and him doubling back for the danger of it, the fervor of the chase, the baton of the tampon a piston, a flash of the fist in pursuit of the impossible plunder, the wonderment from out the eye of the hurricane, from out the beak of the eagle, from offa the spike of the—what do you call it—Sputnik

up there in the dark. That little blip of tin up there in the troposphere.

"Robot power!" he said with a roboty voice. Chirp of the bird.

She swapped him for it. The sleight of the hand. In place of the nose she (clever girl) proffered a brand-new rubber eraser, a slab of red with a slant of a kind you get with a robot. Deal!

Not that it made a fig of a difference a day later, or the day after that, or any many a turn of the earth to the current impasse. The battle of the hatchlings, the glitch in the whirligig, the collision between Martha the Queen of the Tattle and Farrel, the resident criminal. It was the custom—her custom—to savor the nature of the quarrel between the two. To let it simmer. The two suitors, keen, the each of them, to be the only child.

But today was the day of the Smile Contest. Another twenty minutes and the man would appear with the box of goodies, the buttons and the ribbons and the give-aways. It was all she could do to keep the children distracted. In a boil up over the bellwork they were: mugging at the invisible camera, goofing up a smile to set the boys to laughing, chittering on about a prize—a yo-yo, a Slinky, a puppy, a pony. Shameless. Unshushable. And here was a lesson for the ages, O friend of the tender. Break out the Crayolas and color the map of Georgia, thrill to the tick-tock of the time-table, marvel at the innards of a lizard: it ain't nothing but a bucket of air beside a stranger in a snappy blazer and a truck the color of snow.

Even she felt the pull of the clock, the spin of the sweep hand, the catapult across a now they never thought they'd ever see.

Farrel stood to attention as she unfolded the note he'd stolen from Martha. Ad from an issue of Look all mucilaged up onto a sheet of cardstock. Bumper end of a cowboy astride a golden palomino in the blue of a sky branded with a logo: Levi's—Rugged as the men who wear 'em! On the back? A crayon rendition of a... woman? No. Martha's handiwork. Of a dame. No other way to say it. A dame with a set of cherry smackers and a wristful of trinkets and a curve at the waist and the hips and the heels. And hand-lettered, in black India ink inside the ghost of a pencil guide, the title: Miss Connor.

Farrel's contribution to this fever dream of feminine zeal (the improvements he called them) clashed with the stipple of flowers that covered the goldenrod dress, the magenta blooms, the glitter in the ick of the glue at the buckle of the sash, the honest-to-God lipstick on the lips (Martha's mother's brand, Satin Finish, the new Evening in Paris lipstick, there's a bit of Satan in Satin). Ick is right. Not but a couple strokes with a Sharpie was all it took for him to obliterate the scene.

"Tell me about the picture, Farrel." Miss Connor beckoned with the tip of her pen. Thanks to Farrel's repair she stood on the deck of a surfboard now, in outer space, her head in a bubble of a helmet and a ray gun in her hand. "So where am I going?"

"Alpha Centauri."

"To do what?"

"Attack the Centaurians."

"Why? What did they ever do to me?"

"They stole your dog."

"Why would they steal my dog?"

"Cause your dog is special. You got a special dog."

She would save the smile for later. A smile would break the spell. Here was a treat all but hidden from the well-behaved. Brazen he was. Such a brazen child. She pictured the Blue Angels when they paint the sky, one two three strokes, the jets up over the stadium with their plumes booming out behind them.

Back at the back of the class, a stir. Martha Nell Bergdahl with her hand up. The fingers in a waggle. The outrage. The scandal. Miss Connor called her up to testify—the huff and the puff, the head to toe atremble, the knuckles all glisteny and red with the grief of it all, the upshot of which and clear for all to see: Farrel should be punished.

Miss Connor nodded, nodded and traced the outline of the curve of the hip of this Connor person, this intergalactic tart that scootered out over the page. She'd decided long ago the answer to the question of beauty was to refuse the question. "I'm a natural," she told the boys at college when they asked her why she wore no lipstick. "My lips are like cherries," she'd say. "Why would you paint a cherry?" Clever girl. Sassy. The boys at college said as much. She could hear them when they turned away. It pleased her to be—to think of herself as—a provocation, but when they never turned again to press her, to make another go of it, she began to wonder if her way of saying it (a harshness, as if the cherries were bitter) had somehow soured the harvest. Go figure. And by the end of a decade, well, what more was there to say? Was there ever any doubt? There's the fruit you pick and then again there's the fruit you watch and you wait as it ripens and falls.

While the children gnawed away at the board-work (My Country Tis Of Thee in cursive), she fetched from out the hiding place in the closet the treat she promised no, not the children, no, but herself. Promised herself. The print. From off a woodblock. A wave is what it was. A little rectangular ocean she'd happened upon at the Civitan Rummage. A buck and a half, the frame and all. She'd already prepped the wall (clever girl) with a drill, a molly, a screw. You gotta hang it high, right? Outta reach of the heathen. The nubby knuckles and the slickery mitts. The Huns and the Goths, the Visigoths and the Vandals.

Up the wall it slid. She shifted her grip. Cupped her hands to either side to push it higher. Up on her toes even, to where the taut wire at the back of the frame bumped up over the screw. Pling. Into place.

Behold.

In the small of the moment she wondered, not at the wave, but at the maker of the wave. Back in the day of the geisha. Up over the block of wood he hovers. On the neck of a chisel thin as a quill he – with the flat of his thumb – presses. Keen the blade. The every cut a perfect curve. How did they do it, the Japs? She ran a finger up the slope. There. The spray of the sea a solid thing. The surf in a curl at the height of the tsunami, less like a slab of liquid and more like a, like a what? A buttress. A girder bent to the shape of a breaker. Fixed forever now the least little ripple, and up the slope on a roll the rowers, and itty-bitty the boatsmen, and off, and away, in the distance, the snow at the top of the tiny volcano. A nudge. A nudge again to square it, to true it up. There you go. That'll do it. The fast of it all. To hold it – for the time being – fast.

Oh Miss Connor. Beauty is a flower but only so an hour. Even her shoes, so sassy the day she bought 'em – the stilettos, the strap at the ankle, the red leather button – betrayed her. Set her apart. Out and about of late, on the curb, at the crosswalk, in the press of the shoppers she caught it, from out the corner of her eye, the difference. Now the button a bloom, a fleur-de-lis. And the heels. A millimeter shorter. And rounder the toe. There'd been a change in the style she missed, something the new girls, they'd picked up on it, all of them, overnight, and now it was her who was out of step.

Not that it mattered to be a bit off. To grade on the curve. You grade on the curve. And thirty's a curve enough, in on the curve enough to call it – give or take a turn of the earth – young. She ran a hand over the hip and down the seam of the skirt to what? Settle the pleat? Buff the hand? Static up, from out the weave, another puff of chalk? She shifted from one hip to the other. Into the one foot and then the other the whole of herself she poured. A shoe's a thing you buy to bear the weight, true enough, but to the girls with a shape, a shape to speak of, it's all about the geometry. That's what it is. That's the thing. The shape of the leg.

* * * * * *

And so the morning ripened. And so the minutes ran. And so soon—sooner than they figured—the moment arrived. Ten am and the clouds in a cannonade across the green.

What a stir. Had there ever before been such a thing? A Smile Contest? The children skooched together, squeezed off another millimeter of territory between themselves and the front of the line. It was an honor for Mr. Sammy—for that was the name Miss Connor read from the card he gave her—to travel all this way to meet the children and to share with them a smile. Mr. Sammy smiled and then bowed, a big bow, you know, like in the movies when the butler comes with the silver tray with the little envelop with the telegram that says off to Bombay or we attack at dawn or Renfro was the one, it was Renfro all along. The children laughed when he popped back up to attention. Even Miss Connor offered up a smile, sort of a smile, or more like a sketch of a smile, really, when you think about it, which Farrel did, and frequently, as he traveled with his eyes the landscape of her face. This was the smile she saved for occasions when the outcome was uncertain, the tug at the bow on the gift you may, or may not, depending on your mood, decide to open, the lips together in a line that might could maybe spring up (could you but catch it) into a smile.

    The children giggled as Mr. Sammy made a big show of shouldering the reading table into place at the front of the room. A slab of oak is what it was, donation from a somebody uptown. The top a sheet of amber but the underbelly mottled with buttons and barnacles of gum.

    Along the back wall the kids waited. While the other children cheated and elbowed and kibitzed their way to the front of the line, Farrel sifted backwards, to the rear. It was the custom to assemble from the shortest to the tallest, and a boon to Farrel, him being the second shortest in the class, shorter than the girls even, a distinction for sure, and worth fighting for, were it not for Jimmy, little Jimmy who was—with the red vest and the shiny shoes and that pompadour all spatula-ed up into an Elvisy swell—even shorter. How the girls doted on him. Plucked at his collar, clapped onto that warm little wrist of his, pulled him into line beside them. How they'd hug him, huddle him, cry out when Farrel would burst into the heart of the hoop-de-do to drop a Cheeto down the front of Jimmy's shirt, or thumb at his ear with the Elmer's, or body-check him into the boards. Farrel did not know the word and neither did he have a name of his own to call the hunger that hobbled him so. After all these months of trying to wrestle him into line, Miss Connor had a word for it, more than a word. Ravenous the word. Feral.

    Mr. Sammy popped open the box and reached in to pull out a banner that read—blocky white letters in a bed of blue—SMILE. Below the smile, in letters all loop-de-loopy as a icing on a cake, The American Dental Association. Almost the size of the table, the banner sleeved out over the corners like a fitted sheet. When Miss Connor and Mr. Sammy each took a knee to tug it flush, they bumped heads. Bonk. Like in the cartoons. The kids laughed because it was funny—Miss Connor toppled back onto her can in the center of the floor, Mr. Sammy, ka-pow, onto his back. It was Mr. Sammy made the big impression. For days afterwards Farrel replayed the maneuver in his head. How Mr. Sammy flipped, in a single move, ka-boom, from a crabwalk to a push-up and then pop—to his feet.

    Spry the word Miss Connor would've used if she'd had her wits about her. Which she didn't. She rubbed her forehead as if the konk had hurt, which it hadn't, not really, not with the puffet of hair to cushion the blow, ridiculous hair she'd surrendered, in a moment of weakness, to that pushy woman at the Encore with the Hollywood postcards and her between you and me, sweetie and it's all in the bone structure and the cigarette a stiletto in the pinch of the fingers. A bouffant they called it. A pastry's what it was. She rubbed her head to hide her—truth be told and who could blame her, what with all the kiddies atwitter—face.

Two-handed Mr. Sammy took her by the wrists and pulled her gently upward. How fresh, the starch of the collar, the white of the shirt, fresh like a mimeo the smell of the menthol. Sen-Sen maybe. Pep-O-Mint. Up she rose, up into the shadow of the wall of the chest of Sammy, Mr. Sammy. Up under the eyes looking down from on high.

"I'm so sorry." He lowered his face to a level with hers. Whispered. "Quite a team, eh? The two of us?" He smiled. The smell of tobacco but sweet. She pictured a man with a pipe, mahogany pipe, the bowl in the palm of the hand, the breath in a billow up over the knuckle, the shape of the breath a tangible thing. For the sake of the children she offered up a smile of her own. There we go. Upsy-daisy.

Together they sat, the flyers in hand, the table arrayed with the swag for the winners and the tin buttons for the losers (A Smile For Life, Your Dentist Is Your Friend, Today Is Toothday). One at a time they called the children up to give it a shot, to give it their best, the old college try is the way Mr. Sammy put it. Miss Connor smiled at the joke, the something like a joke they—beyond the reckoning of Farrel—shared between them. How sudden it came to pass. Already they'd become a them.

Mr. Sammy shuffled his chair another inch closer. Leaned over to whisper in Miss Connor's ear. She smiled but looked off, out the window and over the chop of the sand to the monkey bars that burned in the midday sun. She'd always been a clever girl. When the boys bet her a nickel she'd never reach the top, that the bars were too hot to handle (and they were: by three o'clock the tops of the rungs simmered like the tongs of a toaster) she'd smiled. So much smaller then. Little spindle bones. If she'd had wings the wind would've taken her for sure. In her purse (a birthday present, patent-leather red with a silver snap) she'd carried a pair of gloves. White. Cotton. She'd never even tried them on before, but they rode with the purse, right? That was the rule laid down by Mama the day they opened the present. A matched set is what they were—the gloves and the purse and the pearls. The pearls she poked down the mouth of an anthill to see what would happen. An ant volcano was what she'd been rooting for, but nothing much happened, and then it rained, and then she forgot. But the gloves. The gloves a kind of a delicate armor. The boys laughed when she pulled them on. Little Miss Priss they called her.

"I betcha a nickel I make it," she shouted as she climbed. "From eacha you a nickel. Seven nickels." Spry. How spry she was out there, under the sun, back in the day. She'd climbed in such a way as to keep only the hands and the feet in contact with the bars, and when she reached the top, and when they shouted back up at her it wasn't fair, that barehanded's what they meant, she hauled herself onto the uppermost rung, stood upright with her white hands waving at the sky and her saddle shoes balanced on the pair of bars that capped the tower, and shouted down at them you should say what you mean. People should say what they mean.

Side by side, Miss Connor and Mr. Sammy. They each had a scorecard of their own—a list really—of all the students in the class, along with columns for marking points in different categories. Farrel figured as much—he could see them ticking off, with check-marks or circles or whatever, the categories. They call your name. Scuff-scuff you go to the front of the room. Stand at the table. Miss Connor says Smile: one thousand and one, one thousand and two... The kid's got his back turned to the rest of the class, so all you see is the back of his head, and then Miss Connor says okay. Thank you. And off he goes, out the door to recess.

Farrel dropped to his knees and crawled beneath the tables that lined the wall. Here was a private tunnel from the rear of the class to the very border of Farrel-land. Here was the private view beneath the banner that hid the bottom half of Miss Connor and Mr. Sammy.

It was Farrel was the one to see Mr. Sammy move his hand. Beneath the table there. Behind the stack of give-aways and the clipboard with the scores. Lift it. Hover. Then bring it down again to rest on Miss

Connor's knee.

There were these movies they'd watch on the rainy days, when into the cafetorium they'd herd the classes so as to give, for a change, the teachers a recess of their own. While the black air flickered and the projector chittered away and the sleeve and the collar stuck to the body, the teachers in twos and threes would gather at the door to gossip, or slip out to smoke beneath the overhang that hid the dumpsters, or shoulder up to the cinderblock wall at the rear of the cafetorium to lean backwards and to press, as if onto the flank of a glacier, the flat of the back.

There was this one movie, cartoon really, that showed the earth. Farrel played it over and over again as he crouched beneath the table. He puzzled over how the world, and every little part and parcel, was a puzzle of a kind you could—what would be the word? It was take-apartable. Even the earth itself, on the inside, like a melon when you slice it, the ball in the sphere in the bigger then the bigger sphere. Geometry is what it was. Mr. Sammy's hand on Miss Connor's knee, the hand in a cup of a curve to fit the shape of Miss Connor's thigh.

There in the dark Farrel practiced what his smile would be. It didn't, on the inside, feel like a smile, but he knew enough to know it was the teeth they wanted to see. Like a set of Legos: you click 'em just so, into place. He would wait to surprise them, that's what he would do.

"Farrel," Miss Connor would say. "Farrel. You need to smile."

"He's not smiling," Mr. Sammy would say.

"You gotta smile, Farrel."

And then he would do it. He would show them. Big fat nutcracker of a grin. Hold it there while they each of them scratch at the clipboard they'd agreed to share, Miss Connor with her Eversharp Adjustable Point Fountain pen with the safety ink shut-off and the one-strike vacuum filler, Mr. Sammy with the eggshell colored Tommy The Tooth pencil held (what with the right hand busy) in the left hand, at a chunky angle, like a first-grader, like it was a caber toss and him up there at the tick-mark fixing to throw.

They would both of them at the very same moment drop the pencil, drop the pen, rise up out of their chairs and—in the shock of the silence (the kids all breathless with astonishment) proclaim him, with a laugh and a shout and a shower of confetti, King of the Smiles. She would take him home with her. He would be her son. They would live in the van with the ice cream, travel the country pitching Dreamsicles and Chilly Willys and Eskimo Pies to the orphans that hide in the haystacks and sleep in the Teepees the Indians abandon. Up over the school they'd hopscotch in their hovercraft, Major Domo at the wheel, to shower the playground with jelly beans and peppermints and chunklets of bubblegum big as the dominos Granddaddy fingered the day he died.

Farrel waited for Miss Connor to look up from her writing. For them to call out for the next contestant. For the moment to pass. Did Mr. Sammy know that his hand was on Miss Connor's knee? Surely he knew, but think of all the places you place your hand when you don't think about the placing of your hand—edge of a table, handlebar of a bike, in the pocket, out the pocket, up the folds of the pillow. The hands, they got a life apart from the body they belong to, got a power apart from even (to hear it from Miss Connor) the mind they been assigned to. Like the day she got so sick of the boys with their sweaty mitts raking up every bauble in sight; the boys on a roll after recess, bouncing off the walls of the class like a bunch of baboons on the loose, and in she comes:

Enough! she said. Enough already!

The Carter boys dropped the coil of wire they'd tortured into a jump rope. It sprang back into shape and slinkey-ed off under a desk. Eddie dropped the bobby pin he'd plucked from Maggie's bonnet. The boys fishing in the bowl of goldfish stirred, stopped, and Farrel paused. Hovered the palm of his hand above the head of the chipper fella on the cabinet upside the teacher's desk, the bobble-head of Mickey Mantle with the xylophone of a grin. Like a benediction he held it there. The Mick in a quiver there. The class of a sudden quiet.

She swept into the center of the room with her hands up, the palms out, the fingers flung upwards for all to see.

The hand is not a magnet! she shouted, and that was that.

The power of the word! The unscratchable itch! For the next couple days, whenever she turned her back, it was like some kind of Magnetorium, Miss Connors' Room 23. Magnet Hand, the whispered incantation, the kids making like every random book or pencil or bag of chips, shoelace or hairbrush or muffin was made of iron. The wall. The floor. The skull of the kid in the seat behind you. Talk about a wow. To be in possession of a power that pulls the world, and every part of it, up into the hold of the palm of the hand. And here Miss Connor in the hold. And here the hand, and her not a move to stop it. Surely she could—if she was of a mind to—shake it loose.

Farrel crouched in the cavern, steadied himself to hold the pounding in his body at bay, readied up a smile, readied himself up a smile as he beheld, gallant boy, the stranger, the smile of the stranger, and—not but a stroke of a brush in the dark, not but a shadow in the stir of a shadow—the hand.

Ever so gently along the top of her thigh it moved.

Winner - Driftwood Press 2019 Adrift Short Story Contest
Pushcart Prize Nominee 2020
Nominated 2020 Best of the Net
Appeared in Driftwood Press Winter 2020 Issue 7.1

NO LIFE SIGNS : PART 1
by Shay Shivecharan

"There are no life sign readings, captain."

Captain Heller felt her stomach turn, though a stoic expression remained firmly in place. In the last weeks the *Pressman* had encountered enough ships with dead crews she began to think they might be the only ones out there still alive. On the screen before her, a dark hulk of metal moved listlessly in the blackness of space. The ship looked as lifeless as her crew almost certainly was.

"Prepare to dock with the *Icarus*, ensign. We're going aboard."

Ensign Culver answered, "Yessir, initiating docking maneuver." He turned to Lieutenant Reynolds, seated at the next console and said, not quietly enough, "Here we go again. Another walk through the graveyard."

"What was that ensign?" Heller asked.

The young navigator stiffened in his seat. "Sorry, captain."

Heller understood the sentiment, it was the very knot she felt inside. Still, there was duty and with it came protocol. Even she would admit hope was far away, just as Cairo Station was. But this was the bridge, manned by the command crew. Officers, all of them. They were the leaders, they set the example. If hope was to ever return, maintaining order was all they could do until then. Often that meant doing the job, even in the face of the worst fears. Sometimes, though, it meant something different. She had made a command decision when they first encountered the *Yelena*, one she stood by when they found the others. The bridge crew needed a reminder, she thought.

"There is a reason all of you are here. You have not only the requisite training, but also the trust of Fleet Command. The trust of each other. My trust. Please remember that, even as we navigate this situation, as difficult as it may be. The truth is important, but in some circumstances it can also be... overwhelming. In that way, truth can also be *dangerous*."

She remembered something her mother often said: *Not all truths need to be known, and not all need to know the truth.* Heller understood the relationship between truth and control. Six ships found in three weeks, over six hundred dead. No survivors. These facts needed to be controlled.

"Captain, should I prepare a rescue team?" Lt. Reynolds asked.

Rescue was standard, but that hardly seemed practical now. "Not this time, Cal. Assemble the salvage team. Let's get all the viable supplies we can off of that ship. Notify Dr. Talin as well. He will probably want to send someone from his staff to perform a forensic investigation."

"Aye, sir."

***

The door to the *Icarus* opened slowly, as if reluctant to reveal what lay beyond. As they did, the look on Lt. Reynolds' face told Heller the officer had an optimism she couldn't feel. This time there might be *someone* left to tell what was sure to be a harrowing tale, but she couldn't bring herself to have any real hope. No life signs, that was what the sensors said.

"What do you think, Captain?"

"I think we are in over our heads, Lieutenant."

"Sorry, sir, I don't follow."

"It's an old saying from Earth of long ago. It means we find ourselves in a situation we are ill-equipped to handle."

"Aye, sir."

The doors stopped. One by one, Captain Heller, Lt. Reynolds, and the five others that made up their boarding party stepped into the darkness beyond them.

***

Two hours later, Janus Heller sat in her personal quarters making her report. On the console before her were images taken aboard the *Icarus* during the salvage mission. Before her assignment as captain of the *Pressman*, she underwent eighteen months of intense training intended to prepare her for the unique demands of commanding a ship that would spend years away from the Border Stations, exploring the outer regions and scouting new systems for possible jump station development. There was, she learned during that time, much to be prepared for. Mechanical failure, of course, was of great concern. Second to that was illness, followed closely by psychological breakdown. One item that was way down on the list of things that might happen, the one possibility that seemed to diminish in likelihood with each generation of space explorers almost to the point of being mere superstition for her own, was the very scenario Captain Heller believed herself to be faced with at that moment.

The pictures were the same as before, and they told a grim story that part of her refused to believe. Could it really be that humankind, driven to the stars by its oldest suspicion about the universe, a desperate hope that fueled the optimism of the earliest space-goers, was finally confronted with the answer to the ultimate question, *Are we alone?* Had centuries of exploring stars systems without discovering a single trace of intelligent life finally brought them around to this?

The crew of the *Icarus* had been slaughtered. It was the same as what had happened on the other ships: the *Yelena*, *Irvine*, *Dawkins*, *Ulysses*, *Bastion*, and *Oedipus*. Bodies, hundreds of them, had been mutilated quite nearly beyond recognition and if there was any explanation behind it, Heller had yet to determine what it may be. As with the others, a full scan of the ship's outer hull had revealed no sign of attack or damage.

"Judging by the evidence at hand, or lack thereof, there is no suggestion of an attack on the *Icarus*," she said aloud. "Her docking port was undamaged, showing no signs of forced entry. After failed attempts at communication, I decided to board her. Once inside, our investigation was admittedly less thorough than was carried out on the other ships. As expected, the entire crew had expired. We took what supplies we could before scuttling her, though our stores were nearly full from what was taken from the other ships. As to the gruesome death of her crew, the responsible party or event remains a mystery, though there is a single clue, consistent with previous investigations, that our forensics analysis has revealed. No one aside from Dr. Talin and myself currently have this knowledge, which is the presence of an unknown organic material discovered on the remains of every crew member. DNA analysis matches its genetic signature to no previously known form of life, and this suggests an alien origin."

Heller stopped for a few moments to consider this. The computer, she knew, would not include this pause in the log record, but she almost wished it would. The revelation that humans had possibly made contact with a race of beings from another world deserved at least a few moments of contemplation. This was especially true considering the violent outcome of these first encounters.

She continued, "The human race has, over the last eight centuries, discovered hundreds of worlds upon which dozens of permanent settlements have been established. Still, none of them had ever revealed any evidence of intelligent life, much less of any other alien race capable of interstellar travel. This era of boundless expansion has abruptly reached an impasse that leaves in question not only the future of human space exploration, but also that of the human race itself. I have pondered the events of past weeks while at the same time looking over my shoulder, waiting for the unthinkable, yet seemingly inevitable, fate that has befallen so many of my comrades to find us. As for most of the crew, I've chosen to tell them the ships were abandoned, the crews possibly still somewhere awaiting rescue. I see no good reason at this time to complicate their duties and responsibilities with the truth."

It was, she had come to believe, sometimes necessary to tell a different story. How could she know if their fate would be any different from the other ships? Did she, as their captain, have a responsibility to present them with the truth? Or was preserving the sanity of her crew the greater responsibility? Under other circumstances, these questions might have straightforward answers. As it was, there was none for her.

"End report," she said, terminating the log entry.

The computer responded, "Report saved. Would you like to transmit now, Captain Heller?"

"Yes, please. Immediately. Estimated time of arrival?"

"Based on our current location, transmission will reach Fleet Command in thirty-three days, eight hours and thirteen minutes."

Being this far out in deep space meant not having the luxury of a second opinion, at least not for a while. Heller's report on the first ship they discovered, the *Yelena*, was sent weeks ago, but she knew that a response from Command was likely not even on its way yet because they still probably hadn't received the transmission.

What will they think?

***

Ensign Ray Culver rested in his quarters, having just ended his shift. As a second year ensign, he was already growing tired of serving on a fleet ship. When he was very young, it had been his dream to explore the stars. Culver's dad had joined the fleet when he himself was a young man, but those were days of boundless exploration. The stories, the tales of discovery and daring told by his father were what set Ray on the same path. To be among the first to explore new worlds and prepare them for human colonization! The very possibility was exhilarating. Time has a way of changing the mold of possibility, though. Expansion slowed as the burdens of colonization began to demand a different set of responsibilities and roles of Fleet ships and personnel. By the time he entered the academy, cadets were told up front what to expect. Political disputes that had arisen between existing colonies during the last century alone demanded the fleet operate more as a peacekeeping entity than one of exploration, the ideal on which it was first created.

Being out on the frontier was much as he had expected. The voyages were long and the missions rarely anything but mundane. In the twenty-one months he had been on the *Pressman*, there had been only one scientific exploration mission of note. The rest served the needs of diplomacy or military support of some colony or another. He thought of his own son, only two years old, and wondered what stories he would tell him one day. It occurred to him that some of his father's tales of adventure were likely more fiction than fact, concocted to create an illusion of grandeur, to paint a picture of a man whose boy would admire and respect him. Culver knew he would have to embellish far more when his own son asked about what great things he had seen and done during his interstellar travels, about what drew him toward the stars so strongly he left his family behind. He certainly couldn't tell the truth, that would be cruel. Even before a year had passed after marrying Liana, before Harris was born, Culver felt not the pull of the stars, but the insistent urge to get as far away as he could from his new wife and child. He took up his father's legacy as a shield to those who spoke against his decision to leave planetside and be stationed on a Fleet ship. In the end, even his mother came around, especially in the wake of the old man's passing.

The door chime sounded and Culver smiled knowingly.

Right on time, he thought.

The console on the desk in front of him flickered to life and showed the image of a woman. He waited before answering, giving pause to question what exactly it was he was doing. The moment passed quickly as it came, however, without any answer he could make any sense of. If there was one thing that deep space seemed to do, it was challenge his ability to remain morally objective. Without the grounding of the world upon which Culver learned the clear difference between right and wrong, that distinction somehow seemed much less obvious to him.

"Enter," he said as the door slid open. Victoria was attractive, maybe even more than his guilt allowed him to admit. She was older, and outranked him. And like him, she was also married.

"I wasn't sure you'd be up for this," she said as she stepped in.

Neither was I, he wanted to say. Instead he replied, "Are you kidding? This is all I've been thinking about today."

She smirked knowingly. "That definitely isn't true. I know we docked with the *Icarus* hours ago. I know we found her drifting, just like the other ships."

"Yeah? What else have you heard?" Victoria worked on the engineering deck, far from the bridge. He was genuinely curious to know if cracks in the story were beginning to show yet elsewhere on the ship.

"Not much. But people are starting to wonder."

Here it comes, he thought.

She crossed the room and walked right up to him. Her hands found his shoulders before they crossed behind his neck. He met her gaze, saw the plea for honesty in her eyes.

"What really happened to those crews?" she asked.

Ray was a head taller than Victoria, but at that moment felt small and backed into a corner. He'd wanted to tell her the truth, that much was sure.

"We don't know."

"I don't believe you, Ray."

He gently pushed her away and walked over to the viewport, gazing into blackness. "Sometimes I wonder what we're even still doing out here. If there is any chance that we could be next... it just doesn't make sense." He faced her again. "We should be heading back to Cairo Station as fast as we can."

He saw anticipation drawn on her face, she was anxious to finally hear the truth. He'd also been wanting this moment, needing it. Ray didn't spend his off-duty time with anyone from the Command crew, even if he did they were under orders to not discuss the situation under any circumstances. In the beginning it wasn't very hard to keep this confidence, but as the weeks passed that changed. He had been on each boarding party. One dead crew piled onto another and then another, until the weight of it all had become something unbearable. Ray had seen things that changed him, things that altered his very understanding of what it meant to be flesh and bone. He thought of the captain's reminder, her admonition, and tried to push it aside.

Here we go.

He turned back toward the viewport and said, "There is no one out there waiting to be rescued. What she told you and everyone else off the bridge was a lie. A lie created to prevent widespread panic on the ship." He gave a half-hearted chuckle, not because he found any of it funny. "Or at least that's the reason the captain gave us."

"Do you always believe what the captain says?"

He shot her a look. It was like a reflex, he was ready to chastise her for even asking the question. Tori wasn't an ensign, though. She was a lieutenant commander. This was her eighth year on the *Pressman*, her sixth under Captain Heller. She'd already moved past the naivete that still afflicted junior officers such as himself. He suddenly felt embarrassed, and this only upset him more. He had grown to hate so much of the training, the indoctrination of Fleet ethics and ideals, even as he held to them so instinctively. Whatever inhibition remained about breaking his oath left in that moment.

"They're all dead, Tori. Every single one of them." He turned to see her reaction.

"All of them? Are you sure?"

He was sure. He had helped count the bodies.

"Not a single escape pod was missing, from any of the ships. No one made it out alive."

She had no words. Surely she had already suspected the truth, but what a truth to come to terms with! After a few minutes she started with the questions. He told her everything. About how there were pieces of them everywhere, on the bridge, in quarters, in engineering, even in the damn lift. She looked on in horror as he told her how the corridors were red, how in some cases there were no bodies to really speak of, only body parts.

They sat quietly together for a time, holding each other long enough to find a shallow comfort. He cared for her, but she was not Caroline. It struck him that it should take such distance from his wife to realize how much he did love her. Still, it wasn't though not enough to make him change course now. Victoria was there for him in a way his wife just couldn't be.

He carried her to the bed where they forgot their fears as easily as they discarded their uniforms. They both knew what existed between them was not love, but it was the only bridge they had to carry them through to the other side of whatever was happening.

***

Deep inside the *Pressman*, on the medscience deck, Dr. Rene Talin feverishly went over the lab results over and over again, seeking out any possible miscalculation, any mistake he could have made. As he did, his heart raced and his mind struggled to comprehend the implications of what he had discovered. With a nervous hand he wiped the sweat from his brow. He simply couldn't believe what the data was telling him, and yet every test he ran, again and again, yielded the same result.

"Incredible," he said aloud.

The DNA results were consistent with the samples from the other ships. The chemical analysis showed the same biological composition as well. Neither had proved enlightening. It was the last test that made all the difference, one he ran out of exasperation more than anything else. He had focused so much on the *how* and *what* of what happened he didn't even bother to think much about the *when*. Yes, he had a chronology of events stitched together from system logs downloaded from the ships, but it wasn't linear time that interested him any longer.

"Display results of temporal analysis."

A holographic cube, shaped by lines and graphs of data, appeared in the center of the room. Dr. Talin considered what he saw, doing a full circle around the three-dimensional projection.

"And there is nothing we can do to stop it..." he said, his voice trailing off as realization dawned on him.

But I must try, he thought.

With a swipe of the hand the projection ended and Dr. Talin walked out of the room. He had to speak to the captain right away.

...TO BE CONTINUED

Printed in the USA
CPSIA information can be obtained
at www.ICGtesting.com
LVHW071734260424
778546LV00011B/168